"You cou...

Matt announc...

Emily could hardly believe she'd heard him correctly. "M-marry you?"

"Think about it, Emily," he said. "If we're married, the baby will have a father, a nice home and a mother who can afford to stay there and take care of him."

"But, Matt—"

"I know what you're thinking. But, Emily—maybe we wouldn't marry for the conventional reason, but I admire you more than any woman I've ever known. And I think you feel the same about me."

"But, Matt," Emily protested, "you'd be giving me so much, and I'd be giving you nothing. I can't have that."

When he spoke, his voice was strained. "Emily, you *would* be giving me something. I don't want to live alone for the rest of my life. I want a wife and a family again.

"You'd be giving me everything."

Dear Reader,

In the spirit of blossoming love, Special Edition delivers a glorious April lineup that will leave you breathless!

This month's THAT'S MY BABY! title launches Diana Whitney's adorable new series duet, STORK EXPRESS. Surprise deliveries bring bachelors instant fatherhood…and sudden romance! The first installment, *Baby on His Doorstep,* is a heartwarming story about a take-charge CEO who suddenly finds himself at a loss when fatherhood—and love—come knocking on his door. Watch for the second exciting story in this series next month.

Two of our veteran authors deliver enthralling stories this month. First, *Wild Mustang Woman* by Lindsay McKenna—book one of her rollicking COWBOYS OF THE SOUTHWEST series—is an emotional romance about a hard-luck heroine desperately trying to save her family ranch and reclaim her lost love. And *Lucky in Love* by Tracy Sinclair is a whimsical tale about a sparring duo who find their perfect match—in each other!

Who can resist a wedding…even if it's in-name-only? *The Marriage Bargain* by Jennifer Mikels is a marriage-of-convenience saga about a journalist who unexpectedly falls for his "temporary" bride. And *With This Wedding Ring* by Trisha Alexander will captivate your heart with a tale about a noble hero who marries the girl of his dreams to protect her unborn child.

Finally, *Stay…* by talented debut author Allison Leigh is a poignant, stirring reunion romance about an endearingly innocent heroine who passionately vows to break down the walls around her brooding mystery man's heart.

I hope you enjoy this book, and each and every story to come!

Sincerely,

Tara Gavin
Senior Editor and Editorial Coordinator

Please address questions and book requests to:
Silhouette Reader Service
U.S.: 3010 Walden Ave., P.O. Box 1325, Buffalo, NY 14269
Canadian: P.O. Box 609, Fort Erie, Ont. L2A 5X3

TRISHA ALEXANDER
WITH THIS WEDDING RING

Silhouette®

SPECIAL EDITION®

Published by Silhouette Books
America's Publisher of Contemporary Romance

This book is dedicated with admiration and the very best
of wishes to Amber Schalk, a courageous friend who is
fighting the good fight. Thanks, Amber, for reminding
me that we should start each day by counting our
blessings and saying thank-you, and also for all the nice
things you've had to say about my books.
My prayers are with you.

 SILHOUETTE BOOKS

ISBN 0-373-24169-0

WITH THIS WEDDING RING

Copyright © 1998 by Patricia A. Kay

This edition published by arrangement with Harlequin Books S.A.

® and TM are trademarks of Harlequin Books S.A., used under license.
Trademarks indicated with ® are registered in the United States Patent
and Trademark Office, the Canadian Trade Marks Office and in other
countries.

Printed in U.S.A.

Books by Trisha Alexander

Silhouette Special Edition

Cinderella Girl #640
When Somebody Loves You #748
When Somebody Needs You #784
Mother of the Groom #801
When Somebody Wants You #822
Here Comes the Groom #845
Say You Love Me #875
What Will the Children Think? #906
Let's Make It Legal #924
The Real Elizabeth Hollister... #940
The Girl Next Door #965
This Child Is Mine #989
A Bride for Luke #1024
A Bride for John #1047
A Baby for Rebecca #1070
Stop the Wedding! #1097
Substitute Bride #1115
With This Wedding Ring #1169

*Three Brides and a Baby

TRISHA ALEXANDER

has had a lifelong love affair with books and has always wanted to be a writer. She also loves cats, movies, the ocean, music, Broadway shows, cooking, traveling, being with her family and friends, Cajun food, Calvin and Hobbes and getting mail. Trisha and her husband have three grown children, three adorable grandchildren and live in Houston, Texas. Trisha loves to hear from readers. You can write to her at P.O. Box 441603, Houston, TX 77244-1603.

All underlined places are fictitious.

Chapter One

"Ashes to ashes, dust to dust..."

Matt Thompson's heart felt as heavy as the overcast Texas sky. As Reverend Tully's deep voice intoned the words of the burial service, Matt watched the face of the young widow who stood so stoically at the grave site.

Emily...

Her name was a whisper in his mind, as sweet as her smile, as pure as her heart, as beautiful as her spirit. She was so brave...and so alone. It hurt Matt to see her standing there by herself, with no one to comfort her.

If only he could help her.

If only he had the right to stand beside her, to put his arm around her thin shoulders and share some of her pain.

But how could he?

The citizens of San Pedro—most of whom were present today—wouldn't understand. Because, after all, Matt was not a relative. He was Emily's boss. If he acted like anything more, they would talk about Emily, and Emily had suffered enough gossip in the past six months. God knows, Matt didn't want to add to her problems.

So he had to content himself with watching her— the way the wind lifted her dark hair, the tears that shimmered in her soft brown eyes, how she refused to give way to the agony he knew she must be feeling.

Emily...

He loved her so much.

From the moment he'd first seen her, he'd loved her. It was just a little over a year and a half ago. He'd gone to Houston to pick up a load of cargo from Jones Medical Supply, one of his oldest customers, and there she was—the new bookkeeper. Sweet, smiling, cheerful—she'd stolen his heart. From then on, he'd made every excuse he could think of to see her. And when she'd mentioned how much she missed small-town life and how nice San Pedro sounded, he'd offered her a job. That was five months ago.

With a rueful inner smile, he remembered how excited he'd been. He'd spun all kinds of fantasies about what would happen. How she'd get to San Pedro and he'd help her find a place to live. How he'd take her under his wing. How she'd come to depend upon him. How she'd begin to see him as Matt, possible husband, instead of just Matt, employer and friend.

Most of what Matt had envisioned had happened. Emily arrived in San Pedro, and he *had* helped her find a house. In fact, he'd helped her buy a house. She'd used the proceeds from the sale of her family homestead in Alabama, and even though there hadn't been much left after she'd paid her mother's medical bills and funeral expenses, there'd been enough to invest in a little place. It was run-down and needed work, but Matt figured he would help her get the place in shape. If all went well, she wouldn't be living there long, anyway. She'd be marrying him and moving out to his home on the outskirts of town.

And then disaster, in the form of Stephen Pierce, struck. Emily hadn't been in town a month when she'd met him—the handsome, charming son of the town's most prominent citizen—and irretrievably lost her heart.

Matt had berated himself over and over again for not staking out a claim right away, the minute he got her to San Pedro. But he hadn't wanted to rush her, and then it was too late.

A month after meeting Stephen, Emily had married him. And now, scant months after their controversial and contested union, she had lost him.

Remembering the cause of all the trouble, Matt's gaze moved from Emily to Stephen's mother, who stood rigidly apart, refusing to even look at her despised daughter-in-law.

Although Cornelia Pierce had never been one of Matt's favorite people, for most of his forty-four years he had felt a reluctant admiration for her. She was a tough old bird who had withstood a lot of adversity. But that admiration had vanished, chased away by her unrelenting disapproval of Emily and the way she'd tried to make Emily's life miserable.

As the richest landowner in Bernard County, Cornelia wielded a lot of power. She could pretty much call the shots, and not many were likely to cross her. So even though Emily had made some friends in San Pedro, and they'd loyally stuck by her through the worst of Cornelia's fury and threats of retaliation, Emily had still felt the ramifications of her mother-in-law's campaign to discredit her. Folks who would normally have fallen at Emily's feet in an attempt to curry the favor of Stephen Pierce's wife, snubbed her and talked about her. Others who were kinder but still reliant on Cornelia's goodwill simply avoided Emily.

This undeserved treatment by Cornelia had infuriated Matt, but it hadn't really surprised him. Cornelia Pierce was not accustomed to being defied, especially not by her son, who, until the time he'd met Emily, had gone along with whatever she wanted. And what she wanted was for Stephen to marry Brenda Colby, the daughter of Rufus Colby, who owned the ranch that bordered Pierce Ranch to the west and north. Even to outsiders, the match had seemed inevitable. Stephen and Brenda had grown up together, and it was obvious Rufus Colby favored the match, too.

And then along came Emily, who destroyed all of Cornelia's plans. Emily, a penniless nobody, an outsider who brought nothing to the marriage.

Cornelia had been coldly furious when she'd found

out Stephen and Emily had eloped. Afterward, when he brought Emily out to the ranch, Cornelia had told him that as long as he stayed married to Emily he would be on his own. She'd thrown him out, letting him take only his personal belongings and his car.

When Emily confided in Matt, he'd successfully hidden his own misery over the marriage and tried to think how he could best help her. A few days later, he called Stephen in. They'd talked, and Matt had offered Stephen a job, but only after telling Stephen that the first time he saw him hot-dogging he'd be history.

"You're an excellent pilot," he'd said, "and you can be an asset to the company, but I won't put up with you showing off or taking unnecessary chances."

Stephen, being Stephen, had grinned, even as he was agreeing. Matt, still feeling reservations but telling himself everyone deserved a chance to prove he had grown up, contented himself with one last warning. Obviously that warning had not taken.

And now Matt would have to live with the knowledge that if he hadn't given Stephen a job Stephen would probably be alive today.

A sudden shifting and murmuring of the funeral attendees roused Matt from his thoughts, and he saw that Reverend Tully had closed his prayer book. The service was over. People were preparing to leave. Knowing it would now be all right to approach her, he headed in Emily's direction, nodding at acquaintances along the way.

Matt waited at the periphery of the crowd, watching as several dozen people murmured final condolences to Emily before turning away and heading toward their cars. Although he couldn't hear Emily's responses, he saw how she met each person's eyes and smiled her thanks. Admiration and pride flowed through him. Emily might have grown up poor in a small Alabama town, but she had an inborn grace. She was a lady, and as far as Matt was concerned, if Cornelia Pierce had any sense at all, she'd have been thrilled to have Emily as a daughter-in-law. She'd have seen that Emily would be a steadying influence on Stephen, and she'd have welcomed her to the ranch.

Suddenly, jolting him, Cornelia's angry voice cut through the crowd.

"It's all your fault!" she shouted, pushing her way through the onlookers.

Emily, who had been talking to Nate Fenster, one of the weekend flyers who hung around the airport where Matt's charter service and flying school were located, turned to look in the direction of the commotion.

"You killed him," Cornelia accused, finally reaching Emily and glaring down at her from the advantage of her five foot ten to Emily's petite five foot three.

Several of the onlookers gasped, but Cornelia ignored them. "If not for you," she continued, "Stephen would have been out at the ranch where he belonged. He wouldn't have been flying that plane because he wouldn't have been working at that piddling job, and he'd be alive today!''

To Emily's credit, she didn't back away. Nor did she retaliate in kind, although she certainly could have. It wasn't Emily's fault Stephen took a job with Matt. She wasn't the one who had banished him from the ranch.

"I'm so sorry, Mrs. Pierce," Emily said quietly. She reached forward, laying her hand on Cornelia's forearm. "I know how you f—"

Cornelia jerked away as if a snake had struck her. Her voice rose a couple of notches, verging on hysteria now. "You know nothing! You certainly don't know how I *feel*." Without waiting for Emily's response, Cornelia barreled on. "How could you know how I feel? You know *nothing* about me. But I know you. I've always known you. You thought you'd struck it rich, didn't you? You thought once you'd gotten your hooks into Stephen, I'd come around. Well, that's never going to happen. Believe me, you'll never see a dime of the Pierce money. Not one single dime.''

Matt pushed forward. No longer worried about the gossip of the townsfolk—all of whom were now gaping in astonishment and embarrassment—he took Emily's arm and placed it firmly through his own.

Giving Cornelia a hard look, he said, "That's enough, Cornelia." He could feel the tremors in Emily's body, although she kept her head high. "If you want to yell at someone, yell at me. I'm the one who hired Stephen."

Cornelia's green eyes, so like her son's, glittered with fury. Her spare body fairly quivered with the force of her anger. "Stay out of this," she hissed.

If Matt hadn't known how grief-stricken she must be, he would have said more. But he really didn't want to get into a shouting match with Cornelia. So he led Emily away, saying quietly, "C'mon, I'll drive you home."

The tears that trembled in her dark eyes were nearly his undoing. Somehow he held on to his common sense and refrained from gathering her into his arms and holding her close the way he wanted to.

No one tried to stop them or talk to them as they walked across the cemetery grounds and down to the winding road where Matt had parked his Bronco. He helped Emily into the truck, then walked rapidly around to the driver's side and got in. He glanced at her as he inserted the key into the ignition. She stared straight ahead, her face pale, hands clutching at her small, black leather purse.

"You okay?"

She nodded.

He wanted to reach over and take her hand. If they hadn't been in plain sight of several dozen people, he would have. Feeling powerless, he started the truck. As they drove away, he saw Cornelia Pierce, accompanied by Larry Halsey, her ranch foreman, and Walker Nesbitt, her lawyer, coming over the small rise leading to the road. Cornelia stared after the truck, her eyes hidden by dark glasses. But Matt knew if he could see those eyes, they would be filled with hate.

* * *

"Let's go, Cornelia."

Cornelia Pierce shook off Walker Nesbitt's hand. She continued to glare after the departing Bronco, as if by the force of her gaze she could somehow will it into oblivion. That's where she wished that woman—she refused to call her by name, even in her thoughts—would go.

Actually, oblivion was too good for her. Hell. That's where she belonged. Hell. Where, every moment, she would suffer, the same way Cornelia was suffering now, the same way Cornelia would suffer for the rest of her life.

Cornelia's jaw clenched.

Stephen, why? Why did you give up everything for the likes of her? How could you be so gullible? So weak? How could you forget everything we'd worked for, everything we'd planned?

The mute questions pulsed in her brain, refusing to go away. There were no answers. And now there never would be, because the only person who could have explained was no longer there to do it, and never would be again.

Taking a deep breath, Cornelia finally turned around.

Without a word to either of her two companions, she began to walk in the direction of the car that had brought them to the cemetery. As they passed the grave site, she gave it a last, lingering look. Soon the cemetery workers would begin filling the chasm, and her Stephen, her handsome, strong Stephen, would be buried in the earth forever, taking all of Cornelia's hopes and dreams for the future with him.

Several times on the ten-minute drive, Matt started to say something, but each time Emily's silence stopped him. Maybe she would feel he was intruding on her privacy if he tried to draw her into conversation.

Matt remembered how he'd felt when Joan and Laurie—his wife and daughter—had died. All he'd wanted then was to be left alone. Even the attentions of his mother and sister, both of whom he loved very much, hadn't been welcome. It was only later, when the first raw grief had abated, that he'd needed to talk.

A few minutes later, he pulled into the driveway of Emily's house, parking behind her Toyota. "I'll go in with you," he said, turning off the ignition. He half expected her to refuse.

"All right."

As Matt followed her across the porch, he wondered how Stephen had felt about living here. Not that there was anything wrong with the house, other than being small and old, but it was a far cry from the fourteen-room stone-and-cedar ranch house Stephen had lived in all of his life. A house that boasted a housekeeper and a cook, not to mention most of the things money could buy.

But when they entered the living room, Matt was amazed by its warmth and welcoming feel. Emily had done wonders here since the last time he'd seen the place, turning it into a cozy, cheerful home.

Everywhere he looked he saw evidence of what he knew was her handiwork: brightly colored pillows, well-tended plants, framed prints and pretty ruffled curtains, gleaming glass bowls filled with potpourri, stacks of books and—sitting on the front window-sill—a beautiful champagne-colored cat with huge, unblinking blue eyes.

Matt couldn't help smiling. So this was the famous Lorelei that Emily talked about all the time, so named because she was a "real siren, unlike me," Emily had said with a soft chuckle and the shy duck of her head that so enchanted Matt.

He turned to Emily, about to comment on Lorelei, and his smile immediately faded. Emily stood motionless, face stricken, eyes filled with a desolation so agonizing it was painful to see. Her face was completely devoid of color, and as he watched, she swayed.

"Emily," he said gently. "You're exhausted. Why don't you go and lie down?" He'd be willing to bet she hadn't slept more than a few hours since the news that Stephen's plane had crashed had come four days earlier.

When she didn't respond, acted as if she hadn't even heard him, he walked over to her and placed his hands on her shoulders. "Emily. Look at me."

Slowly she raised her dark eyes to his.

"You're exhausted," he repeated more firmly. "You should go and lie down for a while."

Biting her lower lip, she shook her head. "M-maybe later."

He could see it would be useless to insist. "All right, but at least sit down." Leading her to the couch, he helped her off with her coat.

She leaned her head back and closed her eyes.

Feeling more helpless than he'd ever felt in his life, Matt watched her and wondered what he should do. Just as the silence began to make him feel uncomfortable, she opened her eyes and looked at him bleakly. "She hates me."

Matt sighed. "Emily, don't pay any attention to—"

"She took the car, you know."

Matt frowned. "The car?"

"Stephen's Corvette."

Come to think of it, Matt *hadn't* seen the red sports car in the driveway. "When?"

Emily hung her head. "Yesterday. I don't even know when it happened."

"How do you know it was Cornelia? Maybe someone stole the car. Maybe we should report it to the police."

"No. It was her. There was a note taped to the front door. It was from Larry Halsey. He just said he'd picked up the car on Cornelia's instructions."

Matt was incensed. "She has no legal right to that car."

"Actually," Emily said wearily, "I think she does, from something Stephen said once, but you know what, Matt? I don't care. I don't want that car. I never wanted anything like that from her or from Stephen.

I just wanted him.'' Her lower lip trembled. ''I just wanted him,'' she whispered brokenly.

While he was still trying to think what to say, she slowly rose to her feet.

He jumped up, too.

''I believe I will go lie down now,'' she said, not looking at him.

''All right.''

He watched mutely as she turned and walked out of the room. He longed to help her but knew that now she needed to be alone. Seconds later, he heard the soft closing of her bedroom door.

He stood there a few minutes, wondering if he should stay or go. Finally, knowing he would worry about her if he left, he decided he would stay awhile. At least until he was sure she was okay.

Heart heavy, he removed his coat, loosened his tie and walked to the window where Emily's cat still sat staring at him. ''Hey,'' he said softly, scratching her head gently. The cat arched her back and leaned into him.

Cats, dogs and kids, he thought wryly. Too bad he didn't have the same effect on women. One woman, he corrected. One woman. Absently, still petting Lorelei, his thoughts returned to the suffering woman in the bedroom beyond.

What would become of her now?

Would she stay in San Pedro? Would she be able to withstand Cornelia Pierce's hatred and fury now that she no longer had Stephen as a buffer?

It would be tough. Much tougher than it had been

before, because, knowing Cornelia, she would not be satisfied with verbally blaming Emily for Stephen's death. She would retaliate, find some way to make Emily pay for what Cornelia considered her sins.

But if Emily didn't stay in San Pedro, where would she go? She had no family left. She had told Matt all about how her father—a drummer in a rock band—had deserted her mother when Emily was only a year old, stranding them both in New York City, and how Barbara Ann had packed up everything and gone back to Avery, Alabama, where the two of them had lived with Emily's Great-aunt Maybelle, and Barbara Ann had worked as a cashier in the local Piggly Wiggly. Everything had been fine, even after Aunt Maybelle died, but then Barbara Ann had gotten sick and Emily had had to drop out of high school and take care of her until her death from multiple sclerosis a few years back. So now Emily was completely alone.

No, she's not, Matt thought fiercely. *She has me. She'll always have me.*

In that moment, he vowed he would always take care of her. Whether she wanted him to or not, he would look after her and do everything in his power to make life easier for her.

I'll be her buffer. And if Cornelia tries anything, anything at all, she'll have to answer to me.

And someday...maybe someday...

He pushed the half-formed thought away. He would not give voice to it, even silently. Why torture himself? Don't wish for things you can't have, that was his credo.

Besides, it didn't matter if she returned his love. Even if she never did, he would always be there for her.

Always.

Just then, startling him, there was a knock at the outside door. Quickly, hoping the knock hadn't disturbed Emily, he walked to the door and opened it. Nell Hollenbeck, owner of the town's only beauty salon and one of the few people who had befriended Emily, stood there. Her hazel eyes were filled with concern.

"Hi, Matt. I thought you might be here."

He smiled in welcome. Stepping aside so she could enter, he said, "I'm glad you came."

Nell looked around. "Where's Emily?"

He inclined his head toward the back of the house. "Resting."

Nell nodded. "Good. She looked completely wiped out at the funeral." She walked over to the sofa, deposited a small duffel bag on the floor beside it, then sat. "Can you believe that Cornelia? That scene she made at the cemetery was just awful. I despise that woman."

"She's a real piece of work."

"Imagine blaming Emily," Nell continued. "Like she was the one who had indulged and spoiled Stephen all of his life and made him think he could do anything he wanted. Shoot, it was just a matter of time before he cracked up that car or broke his neck skydiving or something."

"I should never have given him a job."

"Matt, don't you go blaming yourself. The accident wasn't your fault. For all we know, it may not have been Stephen's, either."

Matt nodded glumly. He would know nothing until the FAA investigation was complete.

"Poor Emily," Nell said after a bit. "It's so unfair. God. It's bad enough to lose your husband, but to be treated like a pariah afterward is...well, it's *criminal*. Right now I'd be willing to bet there are a hundred people out at the Pierce Ranch, all comforting Cornelia. And that's where Emily should be, too."

Matt scowled. What was there to say?

"Well..." Nell settled back and gave him a half smile. "She's got us."

Matt nodded. "You planning to stay long?"

"I canceled all my appointments for the day and told Rick not to expect me until tomorrow morning. I don't want her to be alone tonight."

"Good. That's good."

"So if you need to go, you can."

"I do have some things that need doing." He didn't, but it was probably better this way. Better for Emily to have a woman with her. Better for him to remove himself from a situation that was fraught with danger, because, after all, Matt was only human.

But even knowing this, he stalled. "Uh, if you need anything later, call me. If I'm not at the office, I'll be at home."

"I will," Nell promised.

No longer able to think of any other reason to remain, he walked to the door.

"Matt?"

He turned. Met her clear gaze.

"I'm glad she has you."

Something in her expression told Matt that Nell suspected his true feelings for Emily. Before he could say or do anything stupid, he just nodded, opened the door and left.

Emily heard Nell arrive, and for a moment, she considered going out to greet her. But she didn't have the energy. She didn't even have the energy to get into bed.

She knew she wouldn't sleep. How could she sleep? How could she ever sleep again, knowing that Stephen was gone forever?

Oh, Stephen, Stephen...

The silent cry came from deep in her soul. How could God have done this? How could He take Stephen, who was so young and so full of life and joy?

Stephen.

He'd been so vivid. His bright green eyes. His thick, chestnut hair. Those deep dimples. His brilliant smile. Everything about him had been larger than life. He was the kind of man who made you feel better just because he was in the same room. He was so filled with optimism, so sure everything in life would be wonderful, he made you feel that way, too, even when you knew life *wasn't* wonderful, that it could pound you with one body blow after another, and usually did.

"Listen, sweetness," Stephen would say when Emily would enter a cautionary word to try to temper his enthusiasm about something, "I know you've had a hard time, but that's all changed now. From now on, life is going to be the best." Then he'd lift her off her feet and swing her around, laughing until she laughed, too. Afterward, he'd kiss her. Hard. And then, before too long, they'd tumble into their bed and love each other.

She looked at that bed now.

Barren and empty.

Just like her heart.

How could she bear it? How could she possibly bear it? How could she continue in a world that didn't contain Stephen?

Oh, God...why didn't I die, too?

The tears she'd so successfully repressed all through the interminable hours since Stephen's death welled over now, a torrent of grief so acute it was as if someone were driving knives into her body.

Somehow she managed to remove her suit jacket and kick off her shoes. Then, like a newly blind person groping through a suddenly darkened world, she stumbled into the double bed that had, until a few days ago, been the scene of such happiness and love.

And there, away from all the curious and pitying eyes, alone the way she would be from now on, she wept and wept until there were no tears left.

Chapter Two

Six weeks later

Emily stood by the printer and patiently waited for the contract she'd just finished typing to print. Brilliant March sunshine poured through the recently washed office windows, gilding everything it touched. Beyond the windows, a Piper Cherokee stood poised for takeoff at the end of the single runway boasted by the San Pedro Airport. The sun bounced off its wings, hurting her eyes.

Beyond the runway, fields of green gradually merged into the rolling hills that characterized this part of central Texas. Soon those hills would be covered with bluebonnets and spring would be fully upon them.

Emily sighed. Spring. It had always been her favorite time of year. Somehow, even in the last and worst years of her mother's illness, spring had always engendered hope. But not this year, she thought sadly. No amount of hoping would change things.

As soon as the depressing thought formed, she tried to push it away, just as Matt had told her to. "That's how I survived losing Joan and Laurie," he'd said. "By accepting and moving on. By concentrating on the things I could change and not on the things I couldn't."

Matt.

How would she have gotten through the past weeks without him? she wondered. He'd been a rock, the best friend she'd ever had, there every time she needed him. Quiet when she needed quiet. Ready to talk when she wanted to talk. And always willing to listen.

She grimaced, thinking of all the hours and hours he'd listened to the same things, over and over again. And he'd never once acted bored or tired of her.

Just then, as if he'd known she was thinking of him, the outer door opened and he strode into the office. His sun-bleached, dark blond hair was ruffled from the wind, and his blue eyes crinkled as he smiled.

"Hey," he said.

"Hey." She gave him an answering smile. It was their standard greeting. "How was the trip?" He had just returned from flying a load of cargo to Brownsville.

"No problems." He shrugged out of his flight jacket, tossing it onto one of the worn leather armchairs flanking Emily's desk.

"That's good."

"How about here? Jimmy report for work today?"

She made a face. "Nope. I had to cancel his lessons." Jimmy Donnelly was their perpetual bad boy. He was one of their most experienced pilots and a popular flying teacher, but he had a serious case of wanderlust, and sometimes he simply didn't show up. Emily didn't know how Diana, his long-suffering wife, stood it.

"One of these days, I'm gonna fire his butt," Matt said, but the words carried no sting.

Emily knew that no matter how many times Jimmy messed up, Matt wouldn't fire him, because Jimmy had three kids and Diana made very little from her home-based sewing and alterations business.

Matt was a big softie, Emily thought affectionately. He genuinely cared about people, and in the time she'd known him, she had never heard him say or do anything to hurt another person.

Not that he was a pushover. He wouldn't take any guff, and the men who worked for him knew it. It was obvious to Emily that they all respected him. "You won't fire him," she said. "You're too nice."

"Got you fooled, don't I?"

Emily grinned. She reached for the contract and handed it to him, watching as he studied it intently. When he'd finished looking it over, she said, "You know, Matt, for weeks now, I've been meaning to thank you.''

"For what?" His blue eyes met hers.

"For everything you've done for me since Stephen's death." She walked over to her desk and sat in her swivel chair.

In an embarrassed gesture, he ran his hands through his hair. "C'mon, Emily, you don't have to thank me."

It was so typical of Matt not to take credit for the nice things he did.

"Yes, I do," she insisted. "I—I don't think I'd have made it these past weeks if it hadn't been for you and Nell."

"That's what friends are for." He sat on the corner of her desk.

"Yes, but even friends get tired of holding someone's hand after a while. But not you. You've been there, whenever I've needed you, and I won't forget it."

He was silent for a long moment. Then, looking directly into her eyes, he said, "I'd do anything for you, Emily."

The expression in his eyes made her heart give a funny little hop. Suddenly embarrassed herself, her gaze slid away.

"I've been meaning to talk to you about something, too," he continued after a few awkward seconds, "but I wanted to wait until you were ready to think about it."

"Think about what?"

"You know, despite Cornelia's threats, you're entitled to Stephen's estate. I don't know what assets he might have had in his name, but I can find out."

Emily shook her head. "No. I appreciate the offer, but I don't want anything from Stephen's mother."

"Emily—"

"No, Matt. I mean it."

"But it's not right that Cornelia—"

"Look, Stephen and I were only married for three months. It's not like we had children or anything."

"That doesn't matter. You were his wife."

"Cornelia Pierce doesn't owe me anything," Emily said stubbornly. "I can support myself." There was no way she'd take a nickel from Cornelia, even if the woman were to offer it, because anything Cornelia gave carried strings.

"I understand how you feel, but Cornelia wouldn't be *giving* you anything. What belonged to Stephen now belongs to you. Don't forget, Texas is a community property state, so, by law, anything that was his is now yours."

Emily shook her head again. "I don't want to discuss this, Matt. I don't care about legalities. I know what's right. It's not right for me to take anything that belongs to the Pierces. And I'm not going to change my mind."

He gave her a long, thoughtful look. Finally he shrugged. "All right, Emily, you win."

"It *is* sweet of you to worry about me, though. It means a lot to me to have you for a friend."

"Yeah, well, I just wish you'd listen," he grumbled, standing.

She lightened her voice. "And since I *am* supporting myself, I'd better quit goofing off and get back to work or my boss might fire me."

Matt grinned, picked up his flight jacket and started toward his office. Stopping just inside the doorway leading to his office, he turned. "Remember, Emily. The offer's open. If you change your mind, all you have to do is tell me."

Matt walked into his office, hung his flight jacket on the hook on the back of his door and sank into the battered swivel chair behind his desk. He propped his long legs on the top of the scarred cherrywood desk he'd bought at an auction twenty years ago when he'd first started his business. Many times he'd thought about replacing the desk, then he'd think, hell, why should he? He wasn't trying to impress anyone, and he was attached to the desk. It was an old friend.

And speaking of attachments, Emily was the most courageous woman he'd ever met. He admired and respected her more every day. Still, she was being foolish when it came to the subject of Stephen's money. That stubborn pride of hers had gotten in the way of her common sense.

Maybe he should look into Stephen's estate despite her objections. What was the harm? At least then he would have a better handle on whether to pursue the subject with Emily. If Stephen had no assets in his name, there would be no reason to try to reintroduce the topic.

But if there *were* assets, then, when Emily was in a more receptive frame of mind, Matt would find a way to make her listen to reason.

He nodded in satisfaction. Yes. That was a good plan. It paid to be prepared.

So tomorrow he'd drive over to Fleming, the county seat, and talk to Sally Prewitt, the court clerk. He bet she'd know about Stephen's assets, and if she didn't, she could point him in the right direction.

Smiling, satisfied with his decision, he swung his legs off the desk and settled down to work.

"You're sure?" Matt said.

Sally Prewitt nodded. "I'm sure."

"Well, thanks for looking, Sally. I appreciate it."

"Hey, Matt, anytime."

Matt stifled his disappointment as he drove back to San Pedro. He'd hoped to find that Stephen had a legal share of the ranch or, at the very least, some other asset in his name, but Sally's digging had shown that everything the Pierces owned was in Cornelia's name.

He guessed it was a good thing Emily felt the way she did about not wanting anything from the Pierces, since there was nothing for her to get, anyway.

But by the time he reached the office, he was no longer disappointed. Emily was right. She didn't need anything from Cornelia Pierce. She had her house, her job and her friends.

She would be fine.

Emily hated going home.

Since Stephen died, she'd found any excuse to keep from having to face her empty house. Even Lorelei, who—before Stephen came into Emily's life—had been such wonderful company, couldn't assuage the deep ache of loneliness that was now ever-present.

Emily especially hated eating alone. In the few short months she and Stephen had been together, the best part of the day had been coming home and talking about what had happened that day while they made dinner and then sat down and ate it together.

Now, even though friends like Nell and Matt tried to fill the gap, most nights Emily was alone. But she had gotten very creative in finding ways to postpone the inevitable moment when she would walk into her house and once more feel that sharp pang of loss.

On this particular afternoon, she decided to stay at the office and clean out the files. They sorely needed it. The woman who had served as Matt's office manager for years before Emily came had had no real office experience. She'd just been a friend of his mother's who needed work when her husband died, and Matt, big old softie that he was, had offered her a job.

Before that, he'd done whatever needed doing in the way of clerical work. The sad state of the files reflected both Mrs. Burrows's lack of knowledge and Matt's lack of time. But Emily was determined to correct this problem, and there was no better time than now.

So when Matt emerged from his office at six-thirty, she was kneeling on the floor and up to her elbows in files.

He stopped short. "I didn't know you were still here. What are you doing?"

Looking up, Emily smiled. "Something that should have been done a long time ago. Organizing these files."

He shook his head. "Emily, I don't pay you enough to work this hard."

"You pay me more than enough." They'd had this conversation about her salary before. In fact, two weeks ago Matt had tried to give her a raise, which she'd refused. She'd only been working for him for seven months. No one got a raise after seven months, especially when their starting salary was generous to begin with.

So she'd told him no way. She had no intention of taking charity, especially when she could manage perfectly well on what she made. Hadn't she managed for years on practically nothing?

"Well, I don't pay you to work ten-hour days." He looked at his watch. "Correction. Eleven-hour days. If I'm not mistaken, you came in before seven-thirty this morning."

Had she? She couldn't remember. She only knew that since Stephen's death, she got out of bed the minute she awakened, took a quick shower and ate a quicker breakfast, escaping the house as fast as humanly possible. Otherwise, she might think about all the mornings she and Stephen had made love. All the mornings they'd showered together. All the mornings they'd laughed and talked and planned for the future.

"C'mon," Matt continued firmly. "Leave that stuff until tomorrow. Go wash your face and hands, then I'm taking you out to dinner."

"Matt, you're *always* taking me out to dinner." But her protest was halfhearted.

"I don't call a couple of times a week *always*. Anyway, you're doing me a favor. I hate eating alone."

When he put it that way, how could she say no? Especially when she wanted to go. "All right, as long as it's dutch treat." When he started to protest, she held up her hand to ward off the words. "I mean it, Matt. Dutch treat. Otherwise, I won't go."

He grimaced. "You drive a hard bargain."

"I'll take that to mean yes." She chuckled and got to her feet. "Give me five minutes."

Inside the rest room, she washed her hands, then inspected herself in the small mirror above the sink. She looked better than she'd looked a few weeks ago, she decided, but that wasn't saying much. She was still too pale and much too thin. She'd lost weight since Stephen's death, and she hadn't had much to spare to begin with.

Sighing, she ran a comb through her shoulder-length hair, then quickly applied some blush and fresh lipstick.

When she emerged from the rest room, Matt had his leather jacket on and was sitting leafing through one of the aviation magazines he subscribed to. He looked up. Smiled. "Ready?" His blue eyes reflected his approval as he gave her a quick once-over.

Emily was suddenly glad she'd taken the time to fix herself up a little. Too often lately she hadn't cared about her appearance, and she knew that wasn't good. She reached for her raincoat. In seconds, Matt was standing at her side, helping her put it on. "Thanks, Matt." That was another of the traits she appreciated about him. He was courteous and thoughtful to a fault.

She studied his profile as they walked outside into the cool March night. He was so centered and strong, rarely losing his temper or his even disposition, that sometimes she forgot his life had been touched with a tragedy much greater than hers. Not only had he lost his wife, he'd also lost his daughter. Yet he'd survived. He even seemed, if not wildly happy, at least content with his life. She wondered how long it had taken.

Several times since she'd first found out about them, she'd wanted to ask about his family. All she really knew was that his wife and three-year-old daughter had been killed in a traffic accident on the way back from Dallas, where they'd been visiting his wife's parents. Matt hadn't been with them. He'd had a big cargo job that week, one that carried a tidy profit, so he hadn't gone.

Emily wondered if he thought about the what-ifs. What if he'd gone? What if he'd been driving instead

of Joan? Would he have been able to avoid the accident?

Emily guessed people always wondered what if
they'd done this or not done that. But speculating
changed nothing. If Matt *had* wondered, though, he
seemed past it now.

"So where do you want to go?" Matt said, break-
ing into her thoughts. "Sylvia's or the Diner?"

Remembering all the restaurant choices she'd had
when she'd lived in Houston prior to taking the job
with Matt, Emily smiled. Here in San Pedro, the only
decent choices were Mexican food at Sylvia's or the
Diner, which featured burgers, barbecue and
chicken-fried steak. "You know me. Given a choice,
I'll always pick Sylvia's."

"Good. I haven't had my Mexican food fix for a
couple of days now." He opened the passenger door
of the Bronco. They always rode in his truck when
they went out to eat. Afterward, he'd swing back to
the airport, and she would pick up her car.

It only took five minutes to get to Sylvia's. Since
the whole of San Pedro was only about a half-dozen
miles square, housing a little over three thousand
people, it didn't take very long to get anywhere. Although Emily had grown up in small-town Alabama—and southern towns were very different from
Texas towns—there were lots of similarities between
San Pedro and Avery, one of them being the closeness
of everything and the feeling of community that big
cities could never match. Emily felt safe in San Pedro.
Here people sat out on their front porches and didn't

lock their doors. In Houston, only a fool would leave his house unlocked, and the houses didn't have front porches. Those were the reasons she hadn't hesitated when Matt had offered her the chance to move to San Pedro.

Of course, there were drawbacks to a town like San Pedro, too. The closest movie theater and shopping mall were in Waco, forty-seven miles away. But Emily wasn't the kind to enjoy going to movies alone, anyway, and she'd never been a shopper, so neither deficiency bothered her.

"That looks like Pam and Ben's Suburban," Matt said as they pulled into Sylvia's parking lot.

Pam and Ben Morland were Matt's sister and brother-in-law. Sure enough, when they walked into Sylvia's, the first person they saw was Pam, who was standing in the waiting area with her husband and two teenage sons.

Pam, a tall, pleasant-looking, feminine version of Matt with the same blue eyes and dishwater-blond hair, grinned. "Matt! Emily! Hi."

"Hey, sis," Matt said, giving her an affectionate hug.

Everyone greeted everyone, and Emily thought how much she liked Matt's sister and her family. Ben, Pam's husband, owned the local grain processing plant and was a frequent customer of Matt's. The boys, Ben, Jr., and Michael, were good kids their parents doted upon. So did Matt, who talked about them all the time.

"Let's get a table together," Pam said.

"Do you mind?" Matt asked, turning to Emily.

"No, of course not."

A few minutes later their waiter showed them to a large round table in the corner. Emily sat between Matt and Ben, Jr. Michael was seated next to Matt, then Pam, then Ben. As they settled themselves, Emily could feel Pam's eyes studying her. She looked across the table, and Pam smiled. "It's good to see you again, Emily."

The last time they'd seen each other had been at the funeral.

"How are you doing?" Pam continued, her eyes sympathetic and kind.

"I'm doing okay."

"She's doing great," Matt said. "Her only problem is she works too hard. She'd still be at the office if I hadn't dragged her out and insisted on taking her to dinner."

"I'm *not* working too hard," Emily said.

"I call eleven-hour days too hard," Matt insisted.

"You're exaggerating, Matt. I don't normally work eleven-hour days. The files needed cleaning out and organizing, and you can't do that during normal business hours," she explained.

"Work is good therapy," Ben said.

"Yes, it is," Pam agreed.

"Quit ganging up on me," Matt said. Turning to Michael, he said sotto voce, "Be glad you don't have an older sister. They're bossy."

Michael grinned.

They didn't talk as their waiter filled their drink

orders and brought them baskets of warm chips and bowls of salsa. But once he was finished, Pam turned to Matt. "You know, I was gonna call you later tonight or tomorrow."

Matt ate a chip. "What for?"

"Well, I tried to call Jeff this afternoon and I couldn't get through. So I called the operator and she said the line had been disconnected." Jeff was Matt and Pam's younger brother who lived in California.

Matt rolled his eyes. "Probably didn't pay his phone bill again."

Pam nodded, but her eyes were shadowed with concern.

"Pam," Matt said, "quit worrying."

She sighed and gave him a little half smile. "I know I shouldn't. But think about it, Matt. How long has it been since we've heard from him?"

"I don't know. Couple of months?"

"At least that."

"Well…" Matt shrugged again. "You know Jeff. Sooner or later, he'll call."

Ben laughed wryly. "Yes, like when he needs money."

Pam smiled, and soon the conversation moved on to other subjects, but Emily couldn't help thinking about Jeff Thompson and how lucky he was to have family that cared about him. Too bad he didn't seem to appreciate it.

When she finally turned her attention back to the conversation, Matt and Ben, Jr., were discussing a science project the teenager was currently working on.

Seeing how Matt related to the boys—their easy relationship and how they obviously loved and looked up to him—Emily realized with a pang what a wonderful father Matt would have made. She wondered if, at times like this, he thought about his daughter and how different things would have been had she lived. He must. How could he help but?

Emily didn't know how anyone survived the loss of a child. Losing Stephen was terrible, yes, and she would miss him always, but a child...your own flesh and blood...it had to be the worst pain in the world.

Because her thoughts made her feel sad, she made a determined effort to shake free of them. She didn't want Matt and his family feeling sorry for her. Turning to Pam, she smiled brightly and said, "Matt tells me you're thinking of going back to work." Pam had taught school before marrying Ben and having her children.

Pam grimaced. "Yes. Trouble is, there are no openings in the district, and things don't look promising."

"None at all?" Emily said.

"Nope. People just don't leave. The best I can hope for is that someone will retire." She reached for a chip. "Or maybe I'll have to do something else. What, though, I have no idea."

"You don't *have* to do anything," Ben said.

"I know that, dear heart," Pam said, "but I'm sick of staying home. I'm bored."

Emily thought about how she'd trade places with

Pam in a heartbeat. She had never wanted anything else but to be a wife and, someday, a mother. To make a home for Stephen and their children. She swallowed against the sudden lump in her throat and fought the emptiness that was never far from the surface. She stood abruptly. "I...excuse me...I'm going to the ladies' room."

"Emily," Matt said, "is something wrong?"

Emily forced herself to meet his concerned eyes and smile down at him. "No, of course not. I'll be right back."

Tears pricked her eyes as she hurried toward the safety of the rest room. She was angry with herself. It was weak to be so emotional and thin-skinned that the slightest remark caused her to fall apart.

Reaching the rest room, she opened the door. It had no sooner shut behind her than it opened again, revealing Pam. "I decided I might as well make a visit, too," she said.

Emily murmured something noncommittal and escaped into the nearest stall. She took her time, hoping Pam would be gone by the time she emerged, but when she opened the stall door, Pam was standing there fussing with her hair. Their eyes met in the mirror.

"I upset you, didn't I?" Pam said.

Emily grimaced. "Please don't worry about it, Pam. I'm a mess right now, that's all."

"You just need time."

"I hope so. I know it's hard on my friends." She

gave Pam a rueful smile. "Sometimes I wonder how Matt stands me."

Pam's gaze turned thoughtful. She started to say something, then stopped. For some reason, her expression disturbed Emily, but Emily couldn't have said why. Just when the silence began to feel awkward, Pam smiled and said, "We'd better be getting back. Otherwise the guys might send out a search party," and the moment passed.

Later that night, as Emily lay in bed, she thought again about Pam's comment that she was bored at home. *If I had a home like hers, and a husband and children to take care of, I'd never be bored. I'd be the happiest woman on earth.*

The thought made her feel sad and lonely, and she resolutely pushed it away. She had to stop feeling sorry for herself every time something reminded her of how different her life was now than she'd imagined it would be before Stephen's death.

You know what your problem is, young lady? You need to count your blessings.

That's what her great-aunt Maybelle had always said, even when things had been toughest. "There's always someone worse off than you," she'd add. "Look at old Mrs. Perry, so crippled up with arthritis she can hardly walk. Do you hear her complaining? No, ma'am, you surely don't. Why, every Wednesday she's right there with the other ladies, helpin' out in the food pantry, doin' good in the world, forgettin' about her own troubles."

Great-aunt Maybelle was right, Emily thought with chagrin. *How could I have forgotten?*

Suddenly Emily made a decision. She would look into doing some volunteer work, maybe with kids. She smiled. She loved kids. Why hadn't she thought about doing something like this before?

Because you were too wrapped up in your problems. You weren't ready to think of anything else.

But now she was.

And first thing tomorrow, she'd do something about it.

Chapter Three

But the following day something happened that wiped all thought of volunteer work from her mind. She was going through her desk calendar, looking for a phone number she'd jotted down on one of the pages, when something struck her. She turned the pages more slowly. She couldn't believe what her eyes were telling her. Was it possible? Had she really missed two periods?

Heartbeat accelerating, she flipped the calendar back to February. There was the little notation on the top of the page for February 2, the day she had anticipated her period.

She swallowed. Stephen had been buried on January 24. The week after the funeral was a blur in her mind. Still, she knew she would remember if she had started her period, because she always had terrible cramps that first day. Sometimes the cramps were so bad she had to stay in bed.

Slowly she turned the calendar back to March. There was no notation. Of course not. She always waited until her period actually began before counting off the twenty-eight days until the next one would start.

Oh, my, she thought in wonder. *Am I pregnant? Is it possible?*

She thought back to the night before Stephen left for his ill-fated flight. They had gone to bed early and made love. Afterward, as they lay wrapped in each other's arms, their hearts still beating fast, he'd smoothed her hair back from her face and whispered, "Maybe tonight we made a baby."

She'd smiled. "Oh, Stephen. That would be so wonderful."

"Yeah, it would be. Bet it'll even bring my mother around."

Emily was quiet for a long moment. "Do you think so?"

"I know so. She'll be so thrilled to have a grand-child, she'll forget everything." He idly caressed her breast. "Before you know it, we'll be living out at the ranch."

His words felt like cold fingers around her heart. She couldn't imagine living under the same roof as Stephen's mother. "But, Stephen, I love our little house."

"You'd love the ranch a lot more. Besides, sweetheart, out on the ranch, you'd have all kinds of help and the baby would have a beautiful room and, when he got big enough, his own horse, all the things we don't have now. All the things I want you to have.''

"But I don't want those things, Stephen. All I want and need is you. And our children.''

"*I* want you to have more," he said stubbornly. "And I want our children to have more. I don't want them growing up in a place like this.'' When she stiffened, he quickly added. "I'm sorry, Emily, but you know what I mean. This old house is fine for us, but it's no place to raise a family.''

Although Emily didn't agree, she hadn't argued. After all, what was the point? They were only speculating. If and when she had a baby, if and when his mother mellowed toward them, and if and when they were invited to move out to the ranch, *then* they could make concrete decisions. She just smiled and made a noncommittal sound and burrowed closer into his arms.

"Look, sweetheart," he said a few minutes later. "I understand how you must feel about my mother, considering the way she's treated you and all, but she's not really a bad person. And she *will* be our baby's grandmother.''

"I know.''

"It'll all work out. You'll see.''

Remembering, she closed her eyes. She was afraid to let herself hope. But, oh, a baby! A part of Stephen that she would still have. A child to love and cherish.

Please, God, let it be true. Let me be pregnant. I

*promise, if I am, I'll do everything in my power to
give Stephen's child a good life.*

That night, for the first time since Stephen's death,
she fell asleep with a smile on her face.

Emily couldn't stand it. She was so excited she
simply had to tell someone. So the next day—a Saturday—she called Nell at the salon. "You going to
take a lunch break today?

"Yep," Nell said in her breezy way. "I've got one
to two o'clock free."

"Why don't you walk over to my place, and I'll
feed you?" Emily said. Her house was only two
blocks from Main Street where Nell's salon was located.

"You don't have to do that. Why don't we just go
to the Diner?"

"I want to. Besides, I, um, want to talk to you
about something…in private."

"Oh, okay, then I'll come to your place. See you
a few minutes after one."

Emily was glad Nell hadn't questioned her further.
She didn't want to say anything about her possible
pregnancy over the phone or anywhere in public. Not
until she was sure, anyway.

At five minutes after one, the doorbell pealed.

"Okay, what's up?" Nell said after they'd said
their hellos and exchanged hugs. "What's got you
looking so pleased with yourself?"

Emily grinned. Her heart beat a little faster. "I
think I might be pregnant."

"Emily! Really?"

Finally allowing herself to show some of the happiness the prospect of having Stephen's baby had produced, Emily nodded. "I don't know what else it could be. I've missed two periods. So even though I'm not positive, I think there's a good chance I am."

"I hate to say this, but trauma can cause you to miss a period. When Cassie died, I didn't have a period for three months." Cassie was—had been—Nell's younger sister, and she'd drowned when she was sixteen.

"Really?" Disappointment coursed through her.

"But, hey, a home pregnancy test would tell you for sure."

Emily nodded. "I know. I thought of that, but I didn't want to buy one at the pharmacy. You know, because of Shari."

"Ah." Nell nodded sagely. "Old blabbermouth would have it all over town before you were two feet out the door. Don't blame you, kiddo. But, hey, I've got an idea. Want me to buy a test for you? That won't cause a ripple with Shari. After all, having another kid is hardly big news for me."

Emily chuckled. Nell already had seven children—three from her first marriage, two stepchildren and two from her current marriage. "That would be great. Are you sure you don't mind?"

"Heck, no. I wouldn't have offered if I'd minded."

"Well, okay, then."

"I'll stop on my way back to the shop. You can pick it up later this afternoon."

"All right."

By now they were in the kitchen, and Nell removed her sweater and sat at the table. Emily took a macaroni-and-cheese casserole out of the oven. It was nicely browned on top, just the way she liked it. She placed the casserole on the table where it joined a salad of mixed greens. "What do you want to drink? Milk, iced tea, water?"

"Just water."

A few minutes later, Emily sat, too.

Nell helped herself; then, hazel eyes thoughtful, she said, "Emily."

Emily looked up.

"How do you plan to handle Cornelia if you *are* pregnant? Will you tell her?"

Nell's question gave Emily pause. All the things Stephen had told her about his mother ran through her mind. How tough Cornelia was. How she'd taken over the ranch when his father died. How she'd taken chances and expanded and built it into the one of the most profitable ranches anywhere, even as other ranchers were struggling.

What *would* Cornelia do if Emily was pregnant? Stephen had said once that his mother would stop at nothing to get her own way.

Those words had chilled Emily then. They terrified her now. Cornelia was powerful, with all kinds of resources that Emily could only dream about. She raised frightened eyes to Nell. "I don't know."

"There's no sense in panicking," Nell said. "First

make sure you really *are* pregnant. Remember, this *could* be a false alarm.''

Emily nodded. Wait and see. That was good advice.

''Later, when you know for sure, then you can decide what to do.'' Nell reached across the table and patted Emily's hand. ''Don't worry, Emily. It'll all work out.''

For the rest of Nell's lunch hour, they talked of other things, but Emily had a hard time thinking about anything except her possible pregnancy. As Nell got ready to leave, she said, ''I'll get that pregnancy test now.''

''Okay.''

''I'll put it in one of the salon bags, because Lucille Atkins is my two-fifteen appointment. And she's getting a perm, so she'll be around most of the afternoon.''

''Thanks.'' Lucille Atkins was Cornelia Pierce's best friend. It would never do for her to see what Emily was picking up.

They said their goodbyes and Nell left. Emily cleaned up the kitchen, then donned her red wool blazer and walked outside. She nodded and smiled at the few townsfolk she encountered on the five-minute walk to Nell's salon.

The bell tinkled as Emily walked in. Three heads turned in her direction: Lucille Atkins, head encased in plastic covering; Nell, who stood at the shampoo station working on a customer; and the customer, who Emily belatedly recognized as a teacher from the consolidated high school that served this part of the county.

"Hi, Emily," Nell said. "Glad you stopped by. I've got that moisturizer you asked for." She smiled.

"Oh, good," Emily said smoothly. "I was hoping you did." She finally turned to Lucille Atkins. "Hello, Mrs. Atkins."

"Emily," Lucille Atkins said frostily. She didn't smile.

Emily told herself not to care, but being a naturally friendly person who was predisposed to like everyone and wanted everyone to like her in return, Lucille's less-than-cordial greeting made her feel awkward. *Lord knows, you should be used to it.*

"Just let me finish shampooing Greta and I'll get it," Nell said.

Emily nodded and sat on a stool. She avoided Lucille's eyes, but she could feel the woman watching her.

Nell kept up a stream of chatter as she finished with her customer, then, wrapping the woman's head in a towel, she said to Emily, "I'll get that moisturizer for you now." So saying, she disappeared into her office, reappearing a couple of seconds later with one of the pink plastic bags printed with the name of the salon. "Here you go." She handed the bag to Emily.

"Thanks, Nell," Emily said. Her heart was beating too fast. Although she knew it was silly, she felt as if Lucille Atkins knew what was in the bag.

"Call me later, okay?" Nell said.

"I will. Thanks, again." As she headed for the

door, she glanced at Lucille Atkins, intending to say goodbye, but Lucille's head was bent, and she seemed intent on the magazine in her hands, so Emily said nothing.

Safely outside, she hurried back to her house. Once the door was shut behind her, she removed the kit from the bag. For a long moment, she stared at it. Her heart was beating too fast again.

What are you afraid of?

Emily wasn't sure. She only knew that in the next few minutes she might find out something that would irrevocably change her life.

Taking a deep breath, she headed for the bathroom.

Positive!

Just as she'd stared at the calendar yesterday, Emily's eyes were now riveted to the white stick. It had turned bright blue at the end.

Pregnant.

She was pregnant.

The knowledge reverberated through her, and she closed her eyes and whispered a prayer of thanks. Joy, deep and profound, filled her, yet mixed with the joy was a thread of sadness she couldn't banish. Wouldn't Stephen have been thrilled? And wouldn't it have been wonderful to have him here to share this moment?

Stop that, now. Stop that immediately.

Sighing, Emily disposed of the kit and walked slowly out of the bathroom. She did a quick calculation. Although she couldn't be absolutely sure about when she'd conceived, it had to have been sometime between Christmas and the day Stephen died, so her baby would be due anywhere from late September to mid-October.

Her mother's birthday was October 12. Wouldn't it be lovely if her baby shared that birthday? *Oh, Mom, how I wish you were alive, too. You'd have been so happy for me, I know, and you'd have made a wonderful grandmother...*

Like a dash of icy water, Cornelia's forbidding image flashed through Emily's mind, and Emily was reminded of Nell's question. What *was* she going to do? Should she tell Cornelia about her pregnancy?

The thought of calling Cornelia made Emily shudder. Still, Cornelia was Stephen's mother and the only grandparent Emily's child would have. And she knew it was what Stephen would have wanted.

Besides, she thought ruefully, San Pedro was a small town. She couldn't very well *hide* her pregnancy, so sooner or later Cornelia was bound to find out about it. Wouldn't it be better to tell her up front and get it over with?

You could always leave San Pedro.

The moment the thought formed, Emily rejected it. She didn't want to leave San Pedro. San Pedro was home. This was where she'd met Stephen, where they'd fallen in love, where they'd lived.

And even though lately she had been avoiding being home alone, she loved her little house and knew she would eventually take joy in it again. After her mother died and Emily had moved to Houston and gotten her GED and taken courses at the community college to learn computer bookkeeping, there hadn't been a whole lot of money left from the sale of Great-aunt Maybelle's house. But what there had been, Emily had used to buy her house. The house represented the only financial security she had. She was not going to let Cornelia Pierce drive her away from it, or from San Pedro.

Later, when Emily called Nell as promised and told her how she was trying to decide whether or not to tell Cornelia, Nell said, "You have to make your own decision, of course, but I wouldn't want to be you if you try to keep Cornelia from knowing about this."

Emily worried about what to do all day Sunday, and she was still worrying on Monday morning. At eleven o'clock, Matt finally said something, although Emily was sure he'd noticed her preoccupation hours earlier.

"What's wrong, Emily?" he said quietly.

"Nothing's wrong." Her gaze slid away. She wanted to tell him, but she'd decided that until she'd actually seen a doctor, it would be best not to say a word to anyone other than Nell. Besides, she was leaning on Matt far too much. She needed to learn to stand on her own two feet.

"Are you sure? You seem worried?"

Emily met his gaze again. Made sure her voice was even when she answered. "I'm sure. I'm, you know, just having one of those days again."

He nodded, but doubt lingered in his eyes, and Emily knew she hadn't convinced him.

"Well, I'm always here if you need to talk."

"I know. Thanks, Matt."

After he'd left her alone again, Emily picked up the phone and called Dr. Talbot's office. She would have preferred going to a doctor in Waco, or even in Houston, because everyone in San Pedro went to Dr. Talbot, and if he confirmed her pregnancy, it wouldn't remain a secret long. But if Emily were going to stay in San Pedro, it would be best to go to Dr. Talbot from the beginning, since he would be delivering the baby.

"We can see you tomorrow morning," Dr. Talbot's nurse said when Emily asked for an appointment.

"I hate to miss too much work. Could I possibly come about noon or late in the day?"

"Dr. Talbot's booked solid the rest of the day tomorrow, but he *could* see you at five o'clock today."

"Oh, that would be great," Emily said with relief.

"And what's the reason you're coming in?"

Emily was taken aback, but she recovered quickly. "I, um, it's a female problem."

Thankfully, the nurse didn't press her further. "All right. See you at five."

For the rest of the day Emily tried not to think about the appointment. She didn't want Matt questioning her again, because she didn't like being less than completely truthful. Thankfully, he had a charter at three o'clock that afternoon, one that would keep him overnight, so she wouldn't have to make up any excuses for leaving early.

Somehow she managed to get through the remainder of the day without dwelling on her pregnancy and the problems it had brought about. She got Matt off and took care of everything that needed doing, then closed the office at four forty-five and drove the few miles to Dr. Talbot's office, arriving at five on the dot.

"Hello, Emily," said Patty, Dr. Talbot's nurse cum office manager. "Come on back." She opened the inner door, then, carrying Emily's chart, she led Emily to one of the two examining rooms. The door to the other was closed. Dr. Talbot must be with another patient.

"Now," Patty said as they entered the second examining room and she closed the door, "exactly what kind of female problem is it?"

"Well," Emily said, stomach fluttering nervously, "I've missed two periods and I..." She smiled tremulously. "I think I might be pregnant."

Patty's dark eyes widened. Emily could just imagine what was going through her mind, although she said nothing except, "All right. In that case, undress and put on this gown, then hop up on the examining table. Dr. Talbot will be in shortly."

Emily did as instructed. As Patty had predicted, it was only minutes before Dr. Talbot, a wiry, gray-haired man in his mid-sixties, entered the room.

Fifteen minutes later, a fully dressed Emily sat across from him in his small office.

"You're definitely pregnant," he said. His pale blue eyes reflected concern.

Emily knew he was probably thinking of her newly widowed state and the problems she'd had with Stephen's mother. Even so, his words rekindled her earlier happiness. It was true! She was pregnant with Stephen's child. Suddenly she felt ridiculously close to tears.

"Are you okay?" he asked kindly.

Emily nodded, fighting to get her emotions under control. She gave him a wobbly smile. "I'm just, you know, happy and sad both. I wish Stephen…" Her voice trailed off. *Count your blessings.* She sat up straighter and took a deep breath. "Well, no use wishing. When am I due?"

"I'd estimate around October 15, give or take a few days."

For the next ten minutes they discussed prenatal care, and he told her what vitamins to buy. They briefly discussed when she could have an ultrasound and what she could expect in this first trimester. Then, rising, he took her hand. "Congratulations, Emily. You'll make a fine mother."

"Thank you, Dr. Talbot." She wished she could thank him for his refusal to take sides in the conflict with Cornelia, but she was sure he knew how grateful she was. Voicing her gratitude would probably embarrass him.

"I'll want to see you again in a month."

Emily thanked him again and, feeling dazed, she left. Afterward, she didn't even remember getting into her car and driving home. All she could think about was the baby that was coming in just seven months.

The baby she and Stephen had conceived with such love and hope for the future. The baby that was Stephen's legacy and his final gift to her.

I'll give our child so much love, Stephen. Enough for both of us. I promise.

That night, Emily couldn't fall asleep. Despite her happiness over the baby, she was troubled. She kept thinking about Stephen and what he would say if he were here. She kept remembering the funeral and the raw grief on Cornelia's face. Losing Stephen had hurt her every bit as much as it had hurt Emily.

About two o'clock, she gave up trying to sleep and got up. She walked out to the kitchen and put water on for tea. Luckily she didn't have to try to change habits, because she'd always drunk decaffeinated or herbal tea. While the kettle heated, she took out the photo album she'd started the day she and Stephen were married.

It hurt to look at the pictures Nell had taken. It hurt to see the happiness on both her and Stephen's faces. How young they looked. Emily felt as if the pictures had been taken years ago instead of only five months ago.

Her bottom lip trembled as she studied Stephen's brash smile. In one picture, he was laughing down at her. She remembered that he'd been teasing her. He had loved teasing her.

In another picture, they were toasting each other with champagne. In yet another, he was kissing her.

A tear slipped down her cheek.

The photos represented such a short time in Stephen's life. She imagined Cornelia looking at a life-time of pictures.

In that moment, Emily knew that no matter how much she might want to avoid any further contact with Cornelia Pierce, she had no right to keep the news of Stephen's baby from Stephen's mother.

"Pierce Ranch."

Emily had geared herself to hear Cornelia's voice, but it was the housekeeper who had answered the phone. Adopting her most businesslike tone, she said, "May I speak with Mrs. Pierce, please?"

"I'm sorry, Mrs. Pierce isn't here."

"Oh. Well, um, when do you expect her?"

"Not until Friday. Would you like to leave a message?"

Disappointment coursed through Emily. It had taken courage to pick up the phone and call the Pierce ranch. And now she'd have to sustain that courage for four more days. "Yes, yes, I would. Would you tell her Emily called, and ask her to call me?"

"Emily?" The housekeeper's voice cooled perceptibly.

"Yes, Emily. Stephen's wife. And...and would you please tell her that it's very important?"

"I'll give her the message."

Emily slowly hung up the phone. It was going to be hard to wait, because even if Cornelia had been hostile to her, it would have been much better to get the conversation over with than to worry about it.

Well, then, don't worry about it! she told herself sternly.

"Hah!" she muttered aloud, startling Lorelei, who streaked away in alarm, "that's certainly easier said than done."

The flight home from Argentina was exhausting. It never failed to amaze Cornelia that she could work from sunup till sundown at the ranch, right along with the hands, doing whatever they were doing, whether it was mending fences, branding the cattle, riding the herd, assisting with the calving or any of the other dozens of unending and backbreaking chores, and never get as tired as she did on a long flight.

Well, she'd be home soon, she thought as she looked out the back window of her '87 De Ville and watched the ever-more-familiar landscape roll by. Ned Halsey, the son of her ranch foreman, had made the two and a half hour drive to DFW to pick her up, and she was grateful. She could have taken a puddle jumper to Waco, but she'd always hated those blasted little planes and never more so than now.

At the reminder of the way Stephen died, bitterness and an agony that had not abated in the seven weeks since the accident, flooded her. She closed her eyes and leaned her head back against the seat.

Stephen.

Her beautiful son.

Her strong, smart, *perfect* son.

Gone forever.

The knowledge seared her, burning with an intensity that she knew would never diminish. As long as there was one breath left in her body, she would never get over the loss of Stephen. Never stop missing him. And never stop hating the woman who had caused his death.

Someday, Cornelia vowed. Someday that little slut would pay for what she'd done. Pierces didn't believe in forgiving and forgetting. Pierces believed in an eye for an eye. And even though Cornelia hadn't been born a Pierce, in her toughness and determination, her refusal to accept failure, she was just as much a Pierce as her husband had ever been.

Thinking of Web, she wondered how he'd feel if he could see the ranch today. He'd probably be stunned to see what she had accomplished.

And for what? she thought bitterly. With Stephen gone, there was no one to inherit. No one to keep the family tradition going. No one to care.

"Miz Pierce?"

Cornelia opened her eyes. Saw that they were approaching the entrance road to the ranch. "We're home," she said.

"Yes, ma'am," Ned said.

Ten minutes later, he pulled the Cadillac into the circular turnaround in front of the house, and Cornelia, wincing at the stiffness in her legs, got out. Ned walked around to open the trunk and remove her luggage, and as he did so, Rosella, Cornelia's longtime housekeeper, walked out the front door and onto the porch.

"Welcome home," she said as Cornelia walked up the three shallow stone steps leading to the porch. "Did you have a good trip?"

Cornelia nodded. "It was productive."

Rosella let Cornelia precede her into the house. "Are you hungry? I've got some stew I can heat."

"No." Cornelia removed her jacket and handed it to Rosella. Then she turned her attention to the mail, which sat in a neat pile on the gleaming walnut cabinet that graced the entryway.

"Ma'am?"

"Hmm?" Cornelia said absently, her attention caught by an envelope that resembled a wedding invitation.

"You had some phone calls while you were gone."

Cornelia ran her thumb under the flap of the envelope.

"One of them was from that woman."

Cornelia frowned. "What woman?"

"You know, that woman Mr. Stephen married."

Wedding invitation forgotten, Cornelia slowly turned her gaze to Rosella's. "What did *she* want?" As Rosella explained, Cornelia's jaw hardened. "I knew it was only a matter of time before she tried to get her hooks into Pierce money."

"She told me to say it was very important and that you should call her," Rosella added, her dark eyes filled with the pity that had been there ever since Stephen's death.

"It'll be a cold day in hell before I call *her*," Cornelia spat, her anger growing by the minute. "And if she calls again, here's what I want you to tell her."

Rosella listened quietly, then, like the obedient employee she was, she said nothing more except, "All right, Mrs. Pierce. I'll take care of it."

Chapter Four

All week, Emily had tried not to think about the coming conversation. On Friday, she lost the battle and was on pins and needles all day. She didn't know if Cornelia would call her at the office or wait and call her in the evening. Knowing Cornelia, she probably wouldn't have any qualms about calling Emily at work, so each time the phone rang that day, Emily girded herself for Cornelia's voice.

But when five o'clock rolled around, there had been no call. Relieved to know she could talk to Cornelia in privacy, Emily went straight home, even refusing Matt's dinner invitation.

The phone stayed silent all evening Friday.

Emily told herself Cornelia had probably gotten home late. She would call tomorrow.

Emily stayed close to the house all day Saturday, only leaving for a short time in the late afternoon to buy a few groceries.

When she returned, the answering machine contained no messages. The phone rang once that night—Nell, checking in—but Cornelia didn't call.

She didn't call on Sunday, either.

Or Monday.

Or Tuesday.

Or Wednesday.

Emily sat at her desk late Wednesday afternoon, chewing on a pencil and trying to decide what to do. Should she call the ranch again? Maybe the housekeeper hadn't given Cornelia the message. Because surely, even feeling the way she felt about Emily, Cornelia would be too curious about the purpose of Emily's call to just ignore it. Wouldn't she?

"Every time I pass your desk lately, you're staring off into space."

Emily jumped guiltily. She hadn't heard Matt come into her office. "Oh, sorry." She hastily returned to the on-screen ledger where she was supposed to be entering accounts receivable.

"Hey, it's okay." He sat on the edge of her desk. "That wasn't a criticism."

"If it wasn't, it should have been." She turned to face him. "I was daydreaming."

His steady gaze unnerved her. He said nothing for a long moment. "I know something's bothering you, Emily. I wish you'd tell me what it is."

Emily sighed. The seconds continued to tick by, and finally she blurted out, "I'm pregnant."

Something flickered in the depths of his eyes, there only an instant, then gone. "I see," he said quietly.

"No," she said hurriedly, "you don't see. I'm not upset about being pregnant." Now she allowed herself to smile. "I'm thrilled. What's bothering me is, well, I decided it wouldn't be right of me to try to conceal the fact of my pregnancy from Cornelia, so I—I called her."

Matt's jaw hardened. "And?"

"She was out of town. So I left a message, saying it was important, and asking her to call me, and she hasn't called me back."

"How long ago was this?"

Emily grimaced. "It's been ten days since I talked to the housekeeper."

"And when was Cornelia due back?"

"Last Friday."

Matt shook his head. "Does it surprise you that she hasn't returned your call?"

Emily shrugged. "I guess, in a way, it does. I keep thinking…maybe the housekeeper never gave her the message."

He smiled cynically. "You know, one of the things I like the most about you is the way you always give people the benefit of the doubt. But some people don't deserve it."

"So you think she got my message and has no intention of calling me?"

"Yep."

Emily sighed heavily. "Well, I guess I'll have to call her again, then."

Matt seemed about to say something, then didn't. He finally shrugged. "It's your decision."

"Don't you think I *should* call her?"

"Hell, no. She had her chance. She blew it."

When Emily gave him a pained look, his voice softened. "But, hey, I'm not as nice as you are. You do what you think is right, Emily. This is your decision, not mine."

Emily thought about what Matt had said, but she knew she wouldn't change her mind. Still, she waited until she got home that night before calling the Pierce ranch again. Telling herself not to be nervous or intimidated, she picked up the phone. The same housekeeper answered, and Emily identified herself. "I'd like to speak with Mrs. Pierce. Is she at home?"

"Yes, she is."

Emily waited.

"She told me to give you a message if you called here again," the housekeeper continued.

Something in the housekeeper's voice caused a frisson of disquiet to inch its way down Emily's spine.

"She said she has nothing to say to you. She said as far as she's concerned, you're as dead as her son, so do not call here again."

That night, Matt stayed at work. He tinkered with a World War II vintage B57 bomber that he'd bought at salvage and hoped to bring up to safety standards, and tried to keep from thinking about Emily and her pregnancy. Although he'd never admit it to a living soul, when she'd told him she was pregnant, it had been like a blow to the gut.

He'd fought against the mixture of pain and envy that assaulted him and thought he'd managed to overcome these less-than-admirable feelings quickly enough so that she hadn't noticed anything amiss.

Matt didn't like himself much at the moment. He wanted to be sincerely happy for Emily, because it was obvious how happy she was about the baby she was carrying. But no matter how he tried to pretend all negative feelings had been dispersed, he knew he was lying to himself.

"All right," he muttered, "face it. You're upset because you know that now Emily will be tied to Stephen forever."

Suddenly, as if the simple act of admitting his feelings had erased them, he felt better. Okay, so he was jealous. Big deal. He could live with that. His envy didn't change his feelings for Emily or make him want to help her less. And now, with this new complication, she was going to need help even more than before.

As he worked at loosening a stubborn bolt on the right wing, Matt wondered what Cornelia's reaction would be when she finally did hear the news. Even knowing Cornelia as he did, it was hard to predict what she would do in this case. He guessed it all depended on whether Cornelia believed Emily.

He almost hoped Cornelia *didn't* believe Emily. Because if she did, he couldn't imagine she would allow Emily to raise her grandchild without interference.

He expelled a breath. Whatever Cornelia did, he was sure about one thing. Emily would have to be doubly careful to protect herself from now on.

For the rest of the weekend, Emily was never far from Matt's thoughts. A couple of times, he reached for the phone to call her, then changed his mind. He had no right to interfere. Much as he might wish the situation were different, it wasn't his place to tell her what to do or even to try to influence her decision. After all, he was hardly objective.

So he kept himself busy puttering around his yard and cleaning out the garage, and Sunday night he went to Pam's house for supper. He enjoyed spending time at his sister's, and Sunday was no exception. She'd made a big pot of chili and homemade corn bread—two of his favorites—and the house rang with the noise of the boys and two of their friends. So different from his house, Matt thought, which rang with silence.

Finally Monday morning came. Matt got to the office before seven. He wanted to be there when Emily arrived. He made coffee; then, cradling a steaming mugful in his hands, he stood by the window and watched the sky brighten as the sun climbed from the east.

Morning had always been his favorite time of day. He remembered how, as a kid, he and his father

would set out at four o'clock in the morning to go
fishing, and how they'd watch the sunrise together
from the boat. Those had been good times, real good
times.

Matt missed his father, but in some ways he was
glad James Thompson had died when he did. At least
he'd been spared the pain of knowing about Joan and
Laurie. Laurie had been the sunshine of his life, his
only granddaughter. Even now, Matt could still picture how her blue eyes would light up when she'd
see her "paw-paw." He'd loved Joan, too, telling
Matt once that if he had handpicked a girl for Matt
to marry, he couldn't have picked better than Joan.

As always, thoughts of Laurie and Joan were bit-
tersweet. He wondered if he would ever be able to
think of them without the accompanying sadness.

At 7:35, Matt heard Emily's car. A moment later,
it pulled into view. He waved but wasn't sure if she'd
seen him. Waiting until he heard her enter the outer
office, he walked out to greet her. He was anxious to
know if she'd called Cornelia.

One look at her face told him something had happened, and whatever that something was, it wasn't
good.

"You look like you could use a cup of coffee," he
said.

Emily's attempt at a smile made him ache to put
his arms around her. Instead, he walked to the coffee
bar and poured her a cup of decaf, adding a packet
of sweetener the way she always did. With his emo-

tions firmly under control again, he turned and handed it to her.

"Thanks."

Up close, he could see the dark smudges under her eyes. "Want to tell me about it?"

"I called the ranch again." Avoiding his gaze, she busied herself with straightening things on her desk, although they didn't need straightening.

Matt waited.

Finally she looked up. "She wouldn't talk to me, Matt. She sent a message by way of the housekeeper. *I have nothing to say to you. You are as dead to me as my son, so do not call here again.*"

As Matt listened to the ugly words and saw the pain in Emily's eyes, he wanted to strangle Cornelia. "What a bitch."

Emily said nothing for a long moment. "That may be, but she's still my child's grandmother."

The sad statement weighed on Matt's mind all day. And he knew Emily was thinking about it, too, even though she went about her work efficiently and quietly, the way she always did. As he had many times before, Matt wondered at a deity that would allow so many injustices in the world. Here was Emily, as fine a woman as anyone could hope to know, and all she'd had in her short life had been hardship and loss.

At five o'clock, Matt cleaned off his desk and walked out to Emily's office. She stood at the filing cabinet, her back to him. "Let's close up shop," he said.

She jumped.

"Sorry, I didn't mean to startle you."

"That's okay. I just didn't hear you come in. What did you say?"

She looked better this afternoon, he thought. Her eyes weren't so bleak. And he intended to see that they stayed that way. "I said, let's close up shop. I'm taking you to dinner."

"Oh, Matt, you don't have to—"

"I know I don't have to. I want to."

"No, wait, listen. I—I know you're concerned, but really, I'm okay." She smiled to show she meant it.

"I know you're okay. I'm still taking you to dinner."

"Matt…"

He refused to listen to another word. Finally she quit protesting and did as he'd instructed.

As they walked outside together, she automatically headed for his Bronco. Taking her arm, he turned her in the other direction, toward the hangar.

"Wha—?" The question died on her lips as she realized where they were headed.

"We're going to Hénri's," he said, rolling the ladder over so it would be easier for her to climb up into his favorite plane for pleasure trips—a high-wing Cessna 152 two-seater that he'd finally finished paying off last year.

Once she was inside, he did his external preflight check, starting with the ailerons first—the device that allowed the plane to bank left and right—then moving on to the rudder. When he'd finished there, he checked the gas tank, draining a bit of fuel through the sump drain to make sure there was no water in it. He moved on to the area under the cowl, checking to make sure no oil had spilled over, then looked over the front of the plane and the propellers, again making sure there was no oil spillage.

"Matt, I know why you're doing this," she said when he'd finished his external check and climbed up beside her.

Already starting his internal check, he didn't look at her when he answered. "What's to know? I'm hungry for good Cajun food." He turned the wheel left, then right, watching the ailerons through the window, making sure they were responding.

"You're not fooling me, Matt. You want to take my mind off my problems."

He didn't answer until he'd moved the wheel back and forth and checked the elevators on the tail, then he gave her a sidelong glance. Her dark eyes met his. He grinned. "Is that so bad?"

After a moment, she gave him an answering smile. "You're impossible."

"So they say."

"And very, very nice."

Her words warmed him, and he had to stop himself from looking at her again, because he knew if he did, he might give himself away, and that would be disastrous. The last thing Emily needed was something else to feel guilty about or to worry about, and knowing how he felt about her would do both. So all he said was "Aw, shucks, ma'am," in an exaggerated cowboy drawl, which elicited a soft chuckle and light-

ened the atmosphere—exactly the reaction Matt had
intended.

She watched silently as he completed his preflight
check, and ten minutes later they were airborne.

If Emily lived to be a hundred, she would never be
able to pay Matt back for all his kindnesses, she decided as she settled back into her seat and looked out
the window at the lovely vista slowly spreading be-
neath her. This time of year, the earth was a bright
patchwork of brown and green, intersected by the
winding ribbon of blue that was the San Pedro River.

As the plane climbed higher, she sighed with pleasure. She loved to fly. Not so much in the big com-
mercial jetliners where you were packed in like
sardines and couldn't see much, but in Matt's plane,
where you felt free and light. Where problems and
worries dropped farther away with each mile.

From the day Matt had flown her to San Pedro that
first time, she had loved it. And later, flying with Stephen, had been glorious, although Stephen had scared
her a time or two, because he'd been a bit of a dare-
devil in the air, just as he was on the ground. Matt
wasn't. He was steady, efficient and competent, and
you never felt anything but safe with him.

It took them just under an hour to get to the small,
private airport on the outskirts of Fort Worth. Then it
was another thirty minutes before their cab deposited
them at Hénri's.

Hénri greeted them effusively in his lilting Cajun
patois, his black eyes alight with pleasure. "Me, I am

so glad to see you," He threw his arms around Emily. "Ah, *ma petite,* I am so sorree about your husband."

His warmth caused Emily's eyes to fill. "Thank you, Hénri."

"But tonight we will not think about sad things," he declared, "tonight we will eat and drink and you will be happy, if only for a little while."

And Emily was happy. It was impossible not to be happy when you were at Hénri's. The popular restaurant always attracted a lively crowd. At seven-thirty, a Cajun combo consisting of a woman on washboard and two men—one on the fiddle and one on the accordian—began to play.

The small dance floor soon filled. How could Emily be sad in such a place?

"Thanks for bringing me here, Matt. This is just what I needed." Emily sipped at her iced tea.

Matt smiled and began to eat his crawfish bisque, a specialty of the house. "Me, too."

Taking her cue from him, she picked up her soupspoon. As always, the crawfish bisque tasted like velvet in her mouth. "This is so wonderful."

For a while after that, they didn't talk, just ate their bisque and watched the dancers. Their waiter cleared away their soup bowls and brought them each a small salad. At a neighboring table, a large family was having a birthday party. The birthday girl looked to be about nineteen, bright and innocent and pretty. Emily smiled, watching her as she opened presents and squealed with delight. It must be wonderful to come from such a large family, she thought wistfully.

"They look like they're having fun, don't they?" Matt said.

Emily nodded. "I was just thinking how nice it must be to be part of a big family like that."

Matt said nothing for a long moment. "You were lonely as a child."

She nodded. "Yes, I was. When I was little, I pretended I had sisters and brothers. I even named them. And when I got older and thought about what I wanted out of my life, I promised myself that when I got married I'd never have just one child." She tried to make her voice matter-of-fact, because the last thing she wanted was Matt feeling even sorrier for her. "But life has a way of thwarting the best-laid plans, doesn't it?"

His smile was sympathetic. "You're a young woman. You'll marry again."

She shook her head. "I don't think so."

"You feel that way now, but you'll change your mind later on."

Emily disagreed but decided not to belabor the point. "Do you ever think about marrying again, Matt?"

"Sure, I think about it." His eyes met hers. "I think about it a lot."

She'd had no idea he felt this way.

"You're wondering why I haven't, aren't you?"

She nodded.

"For a long time, I didn't meet anyone who interested me," he said slowly, "and then...when I did...she was involved with someone else."

Emily couldn't think what to say. She wondered whom he was talking about, and possibilities ran through her mind, all of whom she discarded. She couldn't imagine Matt being interested in any of them. Matt was...Matt was *special,* and none of the women she'd thought of were anything but ordinary. She was almost amused by her thoughts. She sounded like a proud mama who didn't think anyone was good enough for her son. But it was the truth. Matt deserved someone exceptional.

"I'm sorry," she finally said.

He shrugged. "That's the breaks. End of story. Now let's talk about something else."

For the remainder of the meal, they kept it light, and by the time their dessert came, Emily was more relaxed than she'd been in weeks. She even felt more philosophical about the episode with Cornelia.

"You know, Matt, I'm not going to worry about Cornelia anymore."

"Good."

"I tried. If she doesn't want to be a part of my baby's life, that's her choice."

"Yes, it is."

Emily speared a strawberry from the top of her cheesecake. "It's sad, though, isn't it? She's so unhappy. You can't help but feel sorry for her."

Matt stirred his coffee. "I don't feel sorry for her."

"Now, Matt..."

"Sorry, Emily. That's the way I feel. The way she's treated you, she doesn't deserve any sympathy."

Emily couldn't helping smiling.

"What?" he said, his own smile quizzical.

"I can always count on you to stick up for me, can't I?"

He reached across the table and squeezed her hand. "You can always count on me, period."

The evening had been a success, Matt decided. Emily had enjoyed herself and relaxed. She had even laughed a couple of times.

He wished he could keep her happy always. If anyone deserved to be happy, it was Emily. Life could be so unfair at times, it made you wonder if there was any rhyme or reason to anything.

"We're almost home," she said.

"I thought you were asleep, you were so quiet."

"No. Just looking out. And thinking."

"Want to share?"

"I was thinking how glad I was you talked me into going tonight. Matt, thanks again. It was wonderful. Exactly what I needed."

"I'm glad you enjoyed it." He wished he could say what he was really feeling. How he'd do anything for her. How he didn't want her to worry. How he'd like to take care of her.

For the remainder of the flight, they didn't talk. Matt concentrated on a smooth landing, and Emily seemed content to just watch.

Once they were on the ground and the plane was safely hangared, Matt walked Emily to her car. He waited until she'd unlocked it. Leaning over, he kissed her cheek. Her skin felt soft, and a faint trace of flowers clung to her hair. Desire, love and a fierce protectiveness surged through him. "I hope you meant it when you said you weren't going to worry anymore."

She smiled. "I'm going to give it my best shot."

He squeezed her shoulder. "If anything does bother you, tell me, okay?"

"Oh, Matt, I appreciate it, but you know, I can't keep burden—"

"It's not a burden. Friends help friends."

"I know, but—"

"No buts. I don't want you worrying about things on your own. I'm here, and like I told you earlier, you can count on me."

She said nothing for a moment; then, startling him, she stood on tiptoe and kissed *his* cheek. "Thanks, Matt. You'll never know how much your friendship means to me."

Later, as he lay in his solitary bed, Matt thought about what a raw deal Emily was getting. Wasn't it bad enough she'd lost both her parents and then her husband? Would it have been too much to ask for her to have a loving, supportive mother-in-law who would be looking as eagerly forward to the birth of her grandchild as Emily was?

In your dreams, Thompson, in your dreams...

Matt knew the best thing for Emily would be for her to leave San Pedro, go somewhere far from the Pierce sphere and have her baby in peace. The thought hurt, but he told himself he loved her enough that he'd rather see her safe than satisfy his own need to have her close to him.

But how could she leave? All her money was tied up in that house, which might be tough to sell. He could help her, of course. He considered the possibility, but quickly discarded it. Emily was too proud to take money from anyone, even him.

Once he realized leaving San Pedro was probably not something Emily would do, he had to admit he was relieved. Even if there was no hope for him as far as she was concerned, at least he could see her and look out for her. He began to think of ways he might make things easier for her.

Several nights later, Pam called and invited him to supper. "Come keep me company," she said. "Ben's gone to a meeting over at the Livestock Commission, and the boys are at the soccer game."

"Don't have to ask me twice."

During the meal, the conversation turned to Emily and Matt told Pam about the pregnancy and what had happened with Cornelia.

"It's not easy raising a child on your own," Pam reflected when he'd finished.

"I know."

"How will she manage financially? It costs a fortune for child care."

Matt nodded. "But I think I've got that solved."

"What do you mean?"

"She can bring the baby to work with her."

Pam stared at him. "Bring the baby to work with her? Matt, that's crazy."

He stiffened. "Why is it crazy?"

"How's she going to get any work done if she has the baby there?"

"She works too hard, anyway. If she needs help, I'll hire someone else."

After a long moment, Pam said softly, "You're in love with her, aren't you?"

"Just because I want to help her?"

"Oh, come on, Matt, this is me, your big sister. I know you. You're in love with Emily."

He thought about denying it, but what the hell. Pam wasn't going to tell anyone. And it would be a relief to confide in someone. He shrugged. "Maybe I am."

"Oh, Matt..."

"What?"

"Nothing. It's none of my business."

He smiled. "When has that ever stopped you?"

She smiled, too, but the smile was tinged with sadness.

"Hey, lighten up. It's not the end of the world."

"I know," she said softly. "It's just that...I love you, and I think you deserve to be happy."

Although he was touched by her obvious concern, he decided to keep it light. "Look, you don't have to worry about me. I'm a big boy. I'll be fine."

"I hope so," she said slowly. "I really hope so."

Chapter Five

Cornelia closed her eyes and lay back in the tub. The hot water felt good on her aching joints. She'd spent most of the day helping old Doc Sweetner birth a colt. It was a difficult delivery, and a good part of the time she'd been down on her knees in the stall, trying to keep Cinnamon, the dam, calm.

I'm too old for this.

The thought was new and disturbing. Until Stephen's death, she hadn't felt old at all. Certainly not anywhere near her sixty-two years.

Today she felt every one of those years...and then some. Suddenly a great weariness spread through her.

Why am I working so hard?

The question was one she'd never before asked herself.

Until two months ago, she'd known the reason. She was working to build Stephen's heritage. The heritage of her grandchildren and great-grandchildren. The heritage of all the generations of Pierces in the future. Now there seemed no point to anything.

Maybe I should sell the ranch.

She examined the unfamiliar idea dispassionately. Rufus Colby would probably leap at the chance to add her holdings to his now that there was no longer any possibility of the two families merging.

She swallowed.

If she *did* sell the ranch, what would she do with herself afterward? She'd come to Pierce Ranch as a nineteen-year-old bride forty-three years ago. She didn't know any other life.

She tried to imagine herself moving away from San Pedro. Going to Dallas or Houston. Buying a condo or a town house. Filling her days playing bridge or golf.

The idea was laughable. She hated big cities, she hated bridge, and she'd never played golf in her life. All she knew was ranching.

Maybe she could travel.

Travel? You hate to travel. After one week, you're ready to come home again.

Her thoughts tumbled in this vein for a long time, until the bathwater became cold enough for her to notice. Desultorily, she thought about adding more hot water, then decided she'd better not. It was time to start getting ready for the evening. Walker Nesbitt and his wife were coming for dinner.

She wasn't sure why she'd invited them. Maybe because she'd been spending too many evenings alone.

Funny how before Stephen's death, she'd never minded being alone. She'd read farm and ranch journals, worked on the books or answered letters. Any one of a dozen things that always needed her attention. Now the house seemed cavernous, every sound magnified, every empty room a reminder of what might have been, and nothing interested her or held her attention for long.

Cornelia had never been an introspective person. She'd been a doer, not a thinker. She'd always been practical, rarely dwelling on the might-have-beens, because she'd learned at a young age that it was a waste of time and energy to chew over things you couldn't change.

Now she seemed to do little else.

Maybe it's time to put you out to pasture.

Thoroughly disgusted with her depressing thoughts, she yanked the stopper out of the tub and stepped out. While she was drying herself, there was a knock on the bathroom door.

"Miz Pierce?" It was Rosella.

"Yes?"

"Miz Pierce, I need to talk to you."

"I'll be out in a minute."

What was so all-fired important that it couldn't wait until Cornelia went downstairs? She finished drying herself and reached for her thick terry cloth robe.

When she walked out into the bedroom, Rosella was standing by the bed, literally wringing her hands.

"Well?" Cornelia said, not bothering to disguise her irritation. "What is it?" She tightened the belt on her robe and walked to her dresser. Picking up her brush, she began to brush her hair.

"You know I went into town to do the weekly shopping this afternoon," Rosella said.

"Yes?"

"While I was there I ran into Patty Alvarez, you know, Dr. Talbot's nurse."

"Rosella, I know who Patty Alvarez is." Finishing with her hair, she put the brush back on her dresser and turned to look at Rosella.

"She told me something I thought you should know," Rosella replied slowly, unruffled by Cornelia's sarcasm. "She said that woman, Mr. Stephen's wife, came into the doctor's office a week or so ago."

Cornelia glared at Rosella. "Didn't I tell you I don't want her name mentioned in this house again?"

"Yes, ma'am, I know, but I figured you'd be mad at me if I didn't tell you about this."

"About *what,* Rosella? Would you please get to the point?" Sometimes she felt like shaking her housekeeper, she was so damned plodding.

Rosella flushed, her dark eyes locking onto Cornelia's. "Patty said Mr. Stephen's wife is pregnant, Miz Pierce. Pregnant with Mr. Stephen's baby."

Emily didn't feel well this morning. She hoped she wasn't coming down with a cold, but she was afraid she might be. Her throat was sore, and her head hurt. She couldn't concentrate on her work and wondered if she ought to go home. But Matt was filling in for Jimmy, who hadn't shown up for work again, and if she left, there would be no one there to answer the phone.

She'd better stay. As she was trying to decide whether to call Dr. Talbot and ask him if she was allowed to take Advil or Tylenol, a dusty red Ford pickup truck careered into the parking area bordering the office. Emily's eyes widened when she recognized Cornelia Pierce in the driver's seat.

Emily barely had time to assimilate this information when Cornelia, dressed in the plaid shirt and worn jeans and boots that were her standard uniform, stalked into the office.

Emily tried not to let her astonishment show. Telling herself she had nothing to fear from Stephen's mother, she slowly rose to her feet. It was easy to see Cornelia was furious. Her eyes glittered dangerously as they settled upon Emily, and there were two bright spots of color on her sun-weathered cheeks.

"Hello, Mrs. Pierce." Emily did her best to ignore the accelerated beat of her heart.

"Is it true?" Cornelia demanded, planting her hands on her hips in a stance calculated to intimidate.

"Is what true?"

But Emily knew. She knew exactly what Cornelia was talking about.

"That you're pregnant, and that you're saying the baby is Stephen's."

Emily stiffened. "Yes, it's true. I am pregnant, but I'm not *saying* the baby is Stephen's. The baby *is* Stephen's."

Cornelia stared at her for a long moment, and it took all of Emily's willpower to keep from looking away.

"I knew sooner or later you'd make your move," Cornelia said, sneering. "You think that now you'll get money from me, don't you?"

"No, Mrs. Pierce. I don't think that at all. I've told you bef—"

"I'm not falling for this old scam. And I demand that you stop saying your bastard is Stephen's!"

"I don't care if you believe me or not." Although her heart was now pounding, Emily refused to fall victim to Cornelia's bullying tactics, because no matter what Cornelia said or did, she couldn't hurt Emily. So her voice was quiet, and her demeanor calm. "I am two and a half months pregnant, and this child is Stephen's. If you choose to pretend it isn't, it will be your loss. And as far as your money goes, you're welcome to it. I want no part of it. It certainly hasn't made *you* happy."

Cornelia's eyes blazed, but Emily met her look steadfastly. The seconds ticked by.

"I can check on your story, you know."

"Go right ahead."

After studying Emily for another long moment, Cornelia snapped, "When are you due?"

"October 15." Emily could see the wheels turning in Cornelia's head. More seconds went by in silence.

"If the child is really Stephen's, as you say, then you must move out to the ranch immediately."

Cornelia had changed tack so fast, it took Emily a few seconds to think how to answer. "That's a kind offer," she said, deciding to be diplomatic, even though Cornelia's words were more command than offer, "but I already have a home."

"That pitiful, run-down place? There's no comparison between it and the ranch. Bad enough that Stephen had to live there. I won't hear of my grandchild being raised there."

Emily just barely managed to hold on to her temper as she reminded herself again that this woman was Stephen's mother and would be her child's grandmother. "You've never even seen my house," she replied with dignity. "It's not pitiful or run-down. It's small, yes, but it's clean and bright and cheerful, and I love it. Stephen and I were very happy there."

"If he was so happy there, why did he call me a week before he died to try to talk me into changing my mind about your marriage?"

Shock, hurt and denial surged through Emily in rapid succession. Stephen wouldn't have called his mother without telling her, would he?

Cornelia watched her, smiling triumphantly. "You didn't know, did you?"

Emily swallowed and struggled to get her emotions under control. Later, after Cornelia was gone, Emily would think about what this meant, but not now. Not in front of Stephen's mother. "I knew Stephen hoped to repair his relationship with you," she said carefully. "He loved you. It hurt him that you'd cut him out of your life."

Although Emily hadn't intended for her words to inflict pain, the smile faded from Cornelia's face, and her eyes filled with a bleakness she couldn't disguise. But within seconds, the bleakness was gone, banished by her steely strength and indomitable will. "So we are agreed, then. Stephen would want his child raised at Pierce Ranch. I will send Larry and Ned Halsey over this weekend to move your belongings."

Emily shook her head. "No, Mrs. Pierce. You misunderstood me. I'm not moving out to the ranch." Searching desperately for some way to convince Cornelia she wouldn't change her mind, she added, "Aside from everything else, I like being close to the office."

"Don't tell me you intend to keep working here?"

"Well, of course. It's how I support myself. It's how I'll support my child."

"If you lived on the ranch, you wouldn't need to worry about that."

"Maybe not, but I prefer to take care of myself."

"What about the baby? Who's going to look after him while you're...*here?* Cornelia's gaze swept the office disdainfully.

"Matt has very kindly offered to let me bring the baby to work with me," Emily replied evenly. She would not get angry. She would not allow Cornelia to draw her into a shouting match.

"Here? You actually intend to bring Stephen's

baby into this smelly, awful place every day? Well, I won't permit it!''

While she was talking, the outer door opened and Matt walked in. "Aren't you forgetting something, Cornelia?'' he said.

Cornelia whirled around. "This is none of your business, Matt Thompson. And I'll thank you to stay out of it."

Emily knew that Cornelia and Matt had butted heads before. She also knew—because Stephen had told her—that Cornelia didn't like Matt. "Matt, it's okay, I can handle this—''

"I'm making it my business," Matt said to Cornelia, ignoring Emily's attempt to calm the waters. "And what you're forgetting, and Emily is too much of a lady to tell you, is that you have no right to tell her what you will or will not permit, because Emily is the baby's mother, not you, and where the baby lives and spends his days is her decision to make, not yours.''

"We'll just see about that," Cornelia spat. "I don't think any judge in his right mind would dispute the fact that I can give Stephen's child a more secure and stable upbringing than the likes of *her*.'' Her glance at Emily was contemptuous.

Matt clenched his fists, and Emily knew that if Cornelia were a man, she'd probably be flattened on the floor by now.

"That's quite enough," he said coldly. "I want you to leave. *Now*.''

"I'll leave, but you haven't heard the last of this.''

She gave Matt one final, furious look before turning back to Emily. "Despite what you might foolishly believe, Stephen's child will *not* grow up here. He will grow up on Pierce Ranch where he rightfully belongs, supervised by his grandmother and a proper staff."

Without waiting for a reply, she stomped out, slamming the door behind her.

Driving too fast, Cornelia headed straight for Dr. Talbot's office. She marched inside and, ignoring the people in the waiting room, demanded to see Dr. Talbot.

"I'm sorry, Mrs. Pierce, but he's with a patient right now," his nurse explained.

"I don't care if he's with the president of the United States. Tell him I'm here."

Cornelia was still smarting from the highhanded way Matt Thompson had ordered her out of his office. He'd be sorry, she vowed. He'd be *real* sorry.

The nurse looked as if she were going to say something else, then must have thought better of it, because she simply sighed, closed the window and disappeared from view.

Cornelia turned to face the waiting room. She recognized most of the people there, all of whom avoided her eyes. A few minutes later, the window slid open.

"Mrs. Pierce?" said the nurse. "Come on back."

The nurse ushered Cornelia into Dr. Talbot's office.

"Have a seat. He said to tell you he'd be with you in a few minutes."

Cornelia sat in one of the two leather chairs flanking his desk. The nurse left, closing the door behind her. Cornelia drummed her fingers on the arm of the chair. She tried to empty her mind, because the more she thought about what had happened back at Matt Thompson's office, the madder she got, and she knew that wasn't good for her blood pressure. Bad enough that Emily was so stubborn, but to have been subjected to Matt Thompson's insults wasn't to be borne. Who did he think he was, talking to her like that?

She stared out the window, her eyes registering the street scene outside, but her brain totally focused on the way Matt had behaved and the things he'd said. He sure had been quick to leap to Emily's defense, just as he had at the funeral. Too quick, to Cornelia's way of thinking. When a man was that protective of a woman, there was usually only one reason for it.

Maybe the baby is really his...maybe she's just pretending she doesn't want to move out to the ranch...maybe it's all an elaborate hoax to reel me in....

Her thoughts continued to churn around and around until the door opened and Dr. Talbot walked in. "What's wrong, Cornelia?" he said without preamble.

"Stephen's wife tells me she's pregnant."

He didn't answer.

"Well? Is it true?"

He sighed. "It's unethical for me to discuss another patient, Cornelia. You know that."

"Now you listen here, Lucas Talbot. If that woman is really pregnant and the child is really Stephen's, I have a right to know."

He pursed his lips and studied her. "She didn't lie to you, Cornelia," he finally said.

"All right, fine. I want to know if there's any way we can tell for certain if Stephen really is the father, then."

Dr. Talbot walked around to the back of his desk and sat in his swivel chair before answering. He looked at her over the top of his glasses. "No, there isn't."

"Why not?" she demanded. "What about DNA? What about blood tests?"

"First of all, there is no blood test that tells us if someone is a child's biological father. All blood tests can do is rule out if someone is *not* the child's father. And," he continued, forestalling her reply, "since Stephen is dead, there's no way to do DNA matching without exhuming his body."

"If that's what it takes, that's what we'll do."

"You don't understand, Cornelia. It's not your decision to make. It's Stephen's wife's, and I can't force her to have the testing done. And neither can you."

Cornelia stared at him. "She doesn't have to know anything about it."

"What do you mean?"

"You know exactly what I mean."

"I won't be a party to—"

"I think you will. Or have you forgotten that I hold the mortgage on your son's place? A mortgage he's four months behind in paying." She let the threat hover there between them, grimly satisfied when she saw the defeated look in his eyes.

Then, very softly, she said, "When that baby is born, you will do exactly as I say. You will obtain a hair sample from the baby, and I will arrange for a sample from Stephen. Then I will have the testing done myself."

Despite Emily's show of courage in front of Cornelia, she was scared. Matt could see the fear in her eyes.

"Emily," he said gently, "it's okay. She can't do anything."

"I know you believe that, but I just can't help it. I'm so frightened, Matt." Tears shone in her eyes, and her voice trembled. "I love it here, and I know my baby will be happy and fine, but…maybe a judge won't see it that way. Maybe he'll look at Cornelia Pierce's money and everything… Oh, God, Matt, what if she can somehow take the baby away from me? M-maybe I should just move out there now, the way she wants."

"Don't even think about it. Don't let that woman frighten you into caving in. That's what she wants. That's how she gets her way in everything, by intimidating and frightening people."

"But maybe this time she's right. Maybe the baby *would* be better off at the ranch."

"No, he wouldn't."

Emily dropped her head into her hands. "Oh, Matt, I wish I knew what to do."

"Listen to me, Emily. Cornelia hates you. If you move out there, you'll be miserable, because she'll do everything she can to undermine you. Hell, you might as well just hand over your child to her, because he will be just as lost to you as if you had." He reached over and squeezed her shoulder. "Come on, Emily. You're a fighter. Well, fight. I'll help you. We'll think of something to do."

She looked up. "But I'm so frightened," she whispered. "I've lost Stephen. I've accepted that. I can't lose my baby, too. I just can't. And Stephen's mother has all the advantages. I have none."

Matt wanted so much to take her into his arms and hold her. He wanted so much to tell her he would take care of her, that she had nothing to fear from anyone. But down deep, a kernel of doubt festered.

Because Emily was right.

Cornelia *was* powerful.

And if she put her mind to it, she might find a judge who would see things her way.

They had to do something.

He had to do something.

He had to find some way to legally safeguard her from Cornelia. And he would. He would if it was the last thing he ever did.

"You have one thing she hasn't got," he finally said. "You have me."

Chapter Six

The first thing Cornelia did when she got home was call Walker Nesbitt.

"Hello, Cornelia," he said. "Emma and I had a nice time last night. She's gonna call you in a coupla days about comin'—"

"I've got a problem, Walker," she interrupted. Briefly, she told him what had transpired that day, ending with her visit to Lucas Talbot's office, although she didn't tell Walker about her ultimatum to Lucas. "And I got to thinking on the way home, what if something should happen to me before that baby is born?"

"Now, Cornelia, nothin' is going to hap—"

"You know, Walker, if I wanted platitudes, I wouldn't have to pay two hundred dollars an hour to get them."

Because Walker Nesbitt wasn't a fool, he simply said, "Sorry. Go on. You were saying?"

"I was saying, if something should happen to me before that baby is born, that woman could lay claim to Pierce Ranch, couldn't she?"

"Well, yes, she could. Hell, Cornelia, *anyone* can lay claim to anything they want, doesn't mean they're goin' to get it."

Cornelia nodded, even though Walker couldn't see the gesture. "Even if the baby *is* Stephen's, I would still want to do something to safeguard the property for him. I sure wouldn't want *her* to have control over it."

"Now that's wise thinkin', Cornelia. I was goin' to talk to you about this subject, anyway, but I figured I'd give you some time first."

"What subject?"

"Changin' your will."

Of course. She couldn't believe she hadn't thought of it. Her will left everything to Stephen.

"Tell you what," Walker said. "Why don't I come on out there tomorrow mornin' about ten? We can sit down and talk about it and figure out the best way to do things."

"All right, but make it nine instead of ten."

At first she thought he was going to protest. Instead, he just sighed and said, "Fine, fine. Nine o'clock it is."

"And, Walker?"

"Yes, Cornelia," he said with exaggerated patience.

"Don't tell anyone about this."

* * *

Matt couldn't sleep.

He tried everything. Counting backward. Counting sheep. Imagining what he'd do if he won the lottery. Nothing worked. Emily's frightened eyes continued to haunt him, and her predicament continued to frustrate him.

Despite all of his assurances to her, he had no idea what he could do that would prevent Cornelia from trying to take Emily's baby away. Short of hog-tying her, he couldn't imagine stopping her from doing anything she was set on doing. He smiled at the image of Cornelia all trussed up. Now wouldn't *that* be something to see?

At four o'clock, he muttered an oath and gave up his futile efforts. Rising, he padded out to the kitchen and filled the coffeepot; then, while it was brewing, he took a quick shower. Twenty minutes later, dressed in jeans and a blue shirt, he stood on the back porch, cradling a mugful of hot coffee in his hands, and looked out at the peaceful predawn landscape.

Dew sparkled in the moonlight, and the night air was chilly. Here in San Pedro, they were just far enough north that the nights didn't get warm until late April or early May. In the woods that bordered his backyard, Matt could hear the rustle of night creatures—squirrels and raccoons and maybe a possum or two, he imagined, although it wasn't unusual for him to spot a deer from time to time.

He'd built his house the first year he and Joan were

married. Except for the electrical wiring and plumbing, he'd done most of the work himself. It was a good house, not fancy, but built to last, with a bright, eat-in kitchen done in the warm yellows and reds Joan had loved. There were three large bedrooms, lots of windows and a big yard that still held Laurie's swing set. It wasn't a bachelor's house. It was a house intended for a family with several children. Sometimes he wondered why he still lived in it. With the shortage of nice homes in the area, he probably could have sold it for a tidy profit.

But he couldn't seem to bring himself to do it. He guessed he still hoped, deep down, that someday he'd have that family.

With Emily...

Forcing his thoughts away from that territory, he focused them once more on Emily's problem. What could he do to help her?

What could he do that would completely stymie Cornelia? Because he knew Stephen's mother. He knew her well. Cornelia never gave up. Once she decided she wanted something, she was relentless.

If she wanted Emily's baby, she would find a way to get him. And Matt couldn't allow that to happen. He had to think of something to stop her. Throw such a roadblock in her path that she would have to give up and Emily could live in peace.

But what?

Okay, tackle the problem logically, the way you do at work. Stand back and look at the situation the way an outsider would look at it. The way the right judge might look at it.

What were the things that Cornelia could offer Emily's child that Emily couldn't? A nicer house was one, of course, but that was a minor problem and easily fixed. Money was another, but Matt didn't think money alone would sway a judge, even one that Cornelia figured was in her pocket. It would be too easy to appeal a decision like that.

No, the big problem and the main thing Cornelia could offer was a better environment for the child— the opportunity for the baby to be raised at home by a mother who did not have to work.

If Emily could somehow stay at home without having to move out to the ranch, that advantage would be taken away from Cornelia.

But how could she? Emily had to work. Otherwise, how would she live?

If Matt could eliminate *that* problem...

Too bad she couldn't move into *his* house. Unfortunately, that was impossible. Even if Matt were to hire her to be his housekeeper, it wouldn't work. People would talk. Emily was too young and too attractive to live in his house with him unless they were married.

Matt froze as excitement shot through him. Of course! That was it. A delighted grin spread across his face. He had the perfect solution.

Now all he had to do was convince Emily.

After a weekend spent worrying and fighting the cold that was now full-fledged, Emily dragged herself out of bed at six Monday morning. She still felt terrible. Her head throbbed, her sinuses ached and her throat felt like someone had rubbed it down with sandpaper.

And why not? she thought. Why shouldn't her physical condition match her emotional one? She might as well face it. She was a complete mess and more frightened than she'd ever been in her life.

Emily was no stranger to adversity. Those eight years of her mother's illness had been tough. They'd had so little money, and caring for her mother was hard work. Emily had been lonely and scared, but somehow she'd managed. Somehow she'd survived. Somehow she'd done what needed doing and built a decent life for herself.

You can survive this, too.

But how?

Short of moving somewhere where Cornelia couldn't find her, changing her name and hiding the rest of her life, what could she do?

If only she wasn't so afraid that no matter *what* she did, it would make no difference to Stephen's mother. That nothing less than complete control of Stephen's baby would satisfy her.

Dear God, please help me.

Despair nearly overwhelmed her, and it was all she could do to shower and dress and get ready for work.

I have to get a grip on myself. There's no reason to panic. It'll be months before the baby is born, and somehow, during that time, I'll find a solution to this problem.

Remembering a book she'd read on how to relieve stress, she sat down, closed her eyes and did deep breathing exercises. Gradually, the tension in her shoulders and neck lessened.

By the time she reached the office, some of her natural optimism had resurfaced, and she felt stronger and better able to face the day. She would figure out something. She had to. Parking her car, she saw that Matt's Bronco was already there.

When she walked inside, he was standing in the doorway that separated his office from hers. He smiled. "Good morning. I've been waiting for you."

She glanced at the clock. It wasn't yet eight. "I'm not late."

"I know. But I've had an idea, and I couldn't wait for you to get here to tell you."

She dropped her purse into her bottom drawer. "An idea about what?"

"I thought of a way we can stop Cornelia cold. A way that will ensure she can't force you to move to the ranch or anything else."

There was an undercurrent of excitement in his voice that was contagious. "You have?" She waited, finally smiling quizzically. "Well, what is it? Are you going to tell me or not?"

His eyes met hers. Another long moment passed. "You could marry me."

She was so startled, she could hardly believe she'd heard him correctly. "M-marry you?"

He grinned. ''Yes. Don't you see? It's the perfect solution. If you marry me, it will negate all of Cornelia's objections and remove every one of her advantages.''

Emily wet her lips. Marry him? Marry Matt? ''I...'' Her voice trailed off.

''Think about it, Emily,'' he said, walking toward her. ''If you're married, she won't have a leg to stand on, nothing to tell a judge if she tries to take your baby away from you. The baby will have a father, a nice home and a mother who can afford to stay there and take care of him.''

''But Matt—'' How could she marry him? They...they didn't love each other.

''I know what you're thinking.'' Coming closer, he reached for her hands. ''Emily.'' His voice was low and urgent. ''I know we wouldn't be marrying for the conventional reason, but I don't believe that really matters. I admire you and respect you more than any woman I've ever known. And I think you feel the same way about me.''

Emily couldn't have looked away if she'd wanted to.

''I think admiration and respect, and the kind of friendship we have, is a much better basis for marriage than romantic love.''

The kindness and sincerity in his voice, the gentleness and regard she saw in his eyes, stirred her deeply. Matt was such a good man. She thought the world of him. And this offer only reinforced her feelings. She couldn't believe he was willing to take such a drastic step to help her.

"Oh, Matt, it's so generous of you to offer to do this for me, but I can't marry you. It...it just wouldn't be fair."

"Emily—"

"No, wait, please let me finish. If...if I married you, it would be so selfish, because you'd be giving me so much, and I'd be giving you nothing. I can't do that, no matter how much I might want to."

"I understand how you might feel that way, but you *would* be giving me something." He released her hands and looked away. When he spoke his voice was strained. "This is hard for me to say, but...I'm lonely, Emily. Ever since Joan and Laurie died, the house has been...so empty."

Emily's tender heart constricted, and she automatically reached out to him, gently laying her hand on his arm.

Slowly Matt turned his gaze back to hers. "I don't want to live alone for the rest of my life. I want a wife and a family again. I'd even like to have more children someday, if you're willing."

"I—I never realized—"

"Look, I didn't tell you this because I wanted you to feel sorry for me. I'm just trying to show you that if you married me, you *would* be giving me something. Something I want very much."

With a little half smile, he slowly touched her cheek. The gentle caress warmed Emily and melted some of the icy fear that had encased her heart ever since Cornelia's abrupt visit the day before.

"Say yes, Emily. I know I'm not Stephen, but we could build a good life together. And your child would be safe from Cornelia forever."

Emily's gaze stayed locked to his as she searched his eyes. The truth of his words was glaringly obvious. She couldn't believe how blind she'd been...and how self-centered. All this time Matt had been hurting, too. And she'd never known, because she was so wrapped up in her own life and her own problems.

Some friend you've been.

But Matt had always seemed so strong, how could she know he was hurting, too? How could she know he might need something from her?

The idea of marrying him, which had seemed so outlandish at first, began to make sense. So what if she didn't love Matt the way she'd loved Stephen? She would never love anyone that way again. That wild, romantic kind of love was a once-in-a-lifetime thing. Respect and friendship and the kind of regard she felt for Matt, those were good, solid emotions that would provide a strong basis for building a successful marriage.

Like Matt, she was lonely, too. She didn't want to spend the rest of her life alone, either. And it would be so wonderful to have Matt to help her raise her child and to stand with her against the Cornelia Pierces of the world. And, as he'd said, she wouldn't just be taking. She'd be giving him something valuable, too.

Her heart beat faster.

It could work.

It really could work.

Placing her hand over his, she held it against her cheek. "You're a good man, Matt. And I think you're right. I think we *could* build a good life together."

The huge grin that split Matt's face sent a rush of happiness through Emily.

"Does that mean you're saying yes?"

Emily nodded slowly. "If you're sure."

Still grinning, he put his arms around her and kissed her forehead. "I've never been more sure of anything in my life."

Although Matt had intended to work on taxes— which were due in two weeks—he spent the day outside instead, tinkering with the B57, because he knew if he stayed indoors, he might do or say something to make Emily change her mind.

The problem was, he was so damned happy he felt as if he might burst. When Emily had said she'd marry him, it was all he could do to keep from crushing her to him. Instead of that chaste kiss on the forehead, he'd wanted to kiss her on the mouth, thoroughly, delving into her sweet depths over and over again.

He'd wanted to say how much he loved her. How he'd *always* loved her. How he would do anything in the world to make her happy. He'd wanted to touch her and hold her and make love to her.

And if he'd done any of it, even given her the *idea* that he wanted to, it would have been disastrous.

He could never reveal his true feelings for her, because if he did, he would scare her off. No, unless and until she came to love him the way he loved her, he would have to be satisfied with what she was able to give him and not push for more.

But it wouldn't be easy.

That night, Emily couldn't sleep. Her brain simply would not shut down. But unlike the nights just past, her thoughts weren't despairing. They were a jumble of hope and excitement, mixed in with a little fear and confusion. She kept asking herself if she was doing the right thing.

What else can I do? I've gone over and over every possible option, and what Matt has suggested is by far the best.

Still, it was scary to realize that in just days she would be Matt's wife with all that status implied. Her heart beat faster as her thoughts veered toward, then shied away from, the area that worried her the most.

She knew it was silly to worry, especially about *that.* Matt was a kind and thoughtful man. She was sure he would be an equally kind and thoughtful lover. He would not rush her or expect her to do anything that would make her feel uncomfortable.

It'll be okay.

She was still telling herself it would be okay the following morning, but for the first time she could ever remember, she felt awkward and uncomfortable with Matt. She was grateful that he spent most of the day in his office, working on the taxes, with the door shut.

They only talked about their decision once, just before noon. He opened his office door and beckoned to her. "I thought it might be best to talk in here. More privacy."

Emily nodded.

"I've canceled the run to Shreveport tomorrow so we can drive up to Waco to get a marriage license, okay?"

"Waco? I thought we'd just go to Fleming."

"Cornelia knows too many people in Fleming," he said, "and I don't want her getting wind of this until we're actually married. Do you?"

Emily hadn't thought of that, but of course he was right.

For the rest of the day, Emily worked in a kind of daze. Saturday afternoon she would be Mrs. Matthew Thompson. It was hard to believe.

As prearranged, Emily was dressed, ready and waiting for him to pick her up at nine the following morning.

Emily hadn't been able to decide what to wear and had finally settled on a pants outfit she'd bought when she and Stephen had been on their honeymoon in New Orleans. The outfit was dark red and silky, with loose fitting pants and a long, matching vest. Under it she wore a cream-colored blouse. The colors were flattering to her fair skin and dark hair and eyes. In it she felt feminine and attractive, now that she had gained back the weight she'd lost when Stephen died.

In fact, the waistband was kind of tight now. Soon she would have to think about maternity clothes, she realized, or at least some transitional outfits with elastic waistbands. Maybe there would be time for her to do some shopping today.

On the dot of nine, Matt's Bronco pulled into the driveway. Emily reached for her jacket and purse, dropped a kiss on the cat's head, saying, "You be good while I'm gone, hear?" and opened the front door. She waved.

Matt, wearing light brown dress pants and a yellow shirt paired with a dark brown sport coat, was already out of the car and walking around to the passenger side.

He smiled down at her. "Ready?"

She nodded, once again feeling shy and awkward.

After helping her up into the truck, he walked back around and got into the driver's seat. He smiled at her again. "You look awfully pretty today."

"Thanks. You look nice, too."

"Special occasion."

She nodded. In that moment, the full impact of what she was doing hit her again. She was going to marry Matt! The fears she'd been successfully suppressing returned in full force.

As if he could read her mind, he reached over and grasped her hand. "It's going to be okay, Emily."

She gave him a tentative smile. "I'm sorry. I'm…just nervous."

"I know." He laughed softly. "I am, too."

And with those words, some of her nervousness disappeared. This was Matt, her best friend. There was nothing to be afraid of.

An hour later, they pulled into the parking lot outside the county clerk's office. Thirty minutes after that, they were the possessors of a marriage license. "The waiting period is seventy-two hours," the clerk informed them. "After that, you can get married anywhere in the county, but the license will expire in thirty days, so don't wait *too* long." She gave them a gap-toothed grin.

Matt and Emily had already decided they would be married Saturday afternoon and drive down to San Antonio for a three-day honeymoon, returning to San Pedro on Tuesday.

After leaving the county clerk's office, they drove to the largest shopping mall in the area and Emily spent a pleasurable couple of hours trying on maternity clothes. Then Matt insisted on buying her something special to wear for their wedding.

"I really don't need a new dress," Emily said. She already felt bad about the money he'd spent on the maternity clothes. "Besides, it's bad luck for the groom to see what the bride is going to wear before the wedding."

"So I won't look," he said.

They went to Dillard's, one of Emily's favorite stores, where she found a beautiful lace dress in a deep shade of rose. It was perfect, she thought. True to his word, Matt wiled away the time it took for

Emily to choose an outfit by looking at CD players in the electronics department.

"All set?" he said, eyeing her package when she rejoined him.

She smiled. It really had felt good to buy something new and pretty. She was glad Matt had suggested it.

"Then it's time for lunch," he said, taking her arm.

They ate at a popular Italian restaurant nearby. Over chicken marsala and salad, they made small talk, avoiding the subject of Cornelia, for which Emily was grateful. She was tired of thinking about Cornelia and especially tired of having Cornelia's threats dictate her every move.

After lunch, they drove slowly back to San Pedro. When they reached Emily's house, she wondered if Matt would expect her to invite him in.

With his uncanny knack of sensing her feelings, he said, "I know you're probably tired, so I'm going to take off, okay?"

Smiling gratefully, she said, "Okay."

He leaned over and kissed her cheek. "I'll see you tomorrow."

The next two days passed slowly for Emily. Doubts continued to plague her, even as she told herself over and over that she was doing the right thing. She'd successfully banish them, but they would come creeping back, keeping her slightly off-kilter.

She kept remembering how Matt had said, "I'd even like to have more children someday, if you're willing." She knew his offer of marriage had been made in the spirit of a mutually beneficial agreement. She needed something, and he needed something. And even though he was a fair and patient man, and would not rush her, eventually he would expect to exercise a husband's full rights.

The thought of making love with Matt—with *any* man other than Stephen—gave her the oddest feeling, part fear, part something else.

Are you sure you know what you're doing?

She prayed she did.

Chapter Seven

The only person Emily confided in was Nell. And she waited until Wednesday night before telephoning her friend. *So she will have less time to try to talk you out of it,* she thought in amusement.

"Are you sitting down?" she said when Nell answered the phone.

"No. Why? Should I be?"

"Might be a good idea."

"Emileeee...what have you gone and done?"

"Nothing yet. It's what I'm getting ready to do tomorrow." She hesitated. Should she explain first or just plunge in and say it?

"Well, come *on,* Emily! *Tell* me! Or do you enjoy teasing me?"

Emily smiled. "Well, now that you mention it, I *do* enjoy teasing you...."

"In a minute I'm gonna drive over there and smack you if you don't spit it out, whatever it is."

Emily laughed. The idea of Nell smacking anyone was ludicrous. Although she had a "sassy mouth"—as she put it—next to Emily, Nell was probably the most nonviolent person Emily had ever met. She'd never even smacked her kids. "Matt and I are getting married tomorrow."

For at least six seconds, there was total silence on the line. Then, cautiously, Nell said, "This is not a joke, right?"

"No, it's not a joke."

"Holy cow! What brought *this* about? No, wait, don't say another word. I'm coming over there. I want to hear everything, from the very beginning, and I don't want to hear it over the phone."

Before Emily could reply, the line went dead. Less than ten minutes later, Nell pulled into the driveway and bounded out of the car.

Emily opened the front door and walked out onto the porch. She grinned. Nell looked like a leprechaun with her red hair, hazel eyes and kelly green pants outfit. "Come into the kitchen. I've got herbal tea and warm banana bread waiting."

"Don't have to ask me twice."

They walked inside and headed for the back of the house.

"All right, tell all," Nell said when they were settled at the kitchen table. Her eyes sparkled with curiosity.

So Emily did, starting with the confrontation with

Cornelia, ending with the trip to Waco to get a marriage license. Throughout, Nell listened quietly. She remained silent for long moments after Emily finished.

"You...you don't approve, do you?"

Nell frowned. "Do you need my approval?"

Emily shook her head. "No, but—"

"Are you going to change your mind if I tell you not to marry Matt? That I think you're making a big mistake?"

"No," Emily said more firmly. "I'm not. I guess I just hoped, well, I'd like to know you wish us well and..." She stopped when she saw the slow grin spreading over Nell's face. "What?"

"Of course I approve. In fact, I think marrying Matt is a terrific idea."

"You do?"

"Yes, I do."

Emily smiled.

"I think the world of Matt," Nell continued. "He's one of the best men I've ever known. And you know how I feel about you." Her eyes danced in excitement. "Oh, Emily, this is perfect!"

"You really think so?"

"Yes, I really do."

"The only thing is..."

"What?"

"I'm...well, I'm just afraid Matt will be disappointed in me. That I won't make him a good wife."

"Emily, that's ridiculous. You'll make Matt an *ex-*

cellent wife, and he'll make you a wonderful husband, not to mention a wonderful father for your baby."

Until that minute, Emily hadn't known how much she really did want Nell's approval. "Oh, Nell, thank you. You don't know how much better you've made me feel."

Nell's grin slowly faded. "Cornelia sure is gonna be mad when she finds out about this little wrinkle."

Emily nodded. "I know. I just hope I'm miles away when it happens."

"I don't blame you. Although I sure would like to be a fly on the wall. I don't think I've ever *seen* anyone blow a gasket."

Emily couldn't help but smile.

"Seriously, Emily," Nell continued, "Cornelia Pierce is not accustomed to losing."

"I know."

"And she doesn't give up just because an obstacle is thrown in her way."

"I know that, too."

Nell took a second piece of banana bread. "So even though it might seem like you've beaten her, my advice would be, watch your back."

Matt put off telling Pam until Friday night.

"Matt! I can't *believe* this!" she said when he'd finished.

"What can't you believe?"

For a moment, Pam was at a loss for words. "I mean, this decision is like, *overnight.* Have you really *thought* about what you're doing?"

He told himself not to get mad. She didn't mean to sound critical. She was just concerned. "I've thought about little else."

"Matt..." Her eyes were filled with doubt. "I don't know... I'm worried..."

"There's no reason for you to worry."

"I can't help it. I—I want you to be happy."

He sighed. "I will be."

"I hope so," she said slowly. But the doubt remained in her eyes.

Ever since the death of their mother, Pam had assumed the role of parent. She'd first tried mothering Jeff, who was fifteen years younger. But it's pretty hard to mother someone who is thousands of miles away. After Joan died, Pam turned her attention to Matt.

In the beginning, Matt had found her attention endearing, but more often lately, her hovering had annoyed him. Hell, she was only three years older than he was. Hardly qualified to mother him. Besides, he didn't need mothering.

"I told you before," he said patiently, struggling not to show his annoyance. "I'm a grown man. Forty-four years old. I can take care of myself."

"I know, but...it's just that I don't want to see you get hurt again."

"And what makes you so sure I will?" Now he made no effort to disguise his feelings. "Thanks for your vote of confidence."

"Oh, Matt, I—I'm sorry," she said quickly, flushing. "If this is what you want, I really am glad for you. You know that."

"Good. Because this *is* what I want."

"In that case..." She put her arms around him and hugged him, and after only a second's hesitation he returned the hug. "I hope you'll be very happy."

That night—the last he'd spend alone—he thought about Pam's reaction to his news. He knew it was a harbinger of things to come. He imagined everyone in San Pedro would be shocked, considering Stephen had only been dead a little over two months. The town gossips would probably have a field day.

He didn't care. No matter what anyone thought or said, he and Emily would make a good marriage.

I'll make her happy.

And if she was happy, then he would be, too.

Saturday dawned clear and mild. About seven, Emily walked out onto her tiny back stoop and took a deep breath of the fresh April air.

She looked around. A male and female cardinal were feeding at the bird feeder she'd hung from a branch of the big chinaberry tree that dominated her backyard. She loved the tree. In the past two weeks, it had started to bloom and now it was covered with pale lavender flowers.

Finished feeding, the male cardinal flexed its wings, its deep scarlet plumage a brilliant contrast to the delicate blossoms and bright new leaves that had sprouted on the branches.

The saint augustine grass was turning green again, too. Everywhere she looked, new life was beginning.

Smiling, she touched her stomach. *And here is the most precious new life of all.* She stood like that for long minutes. It was still too early in her pregnancy for her to feel the baby moving, but she liked touching her stomach. She liked the feeling of connection it brought her. Instead, she moved her hand back and forth, and when she did, the morning sun glinted off her gold wedding band. Her hand stilled, and she stared at the wedding band for a moment, knowing it was time to remove it, but somehow unable to sever this last, visible link to Stephen.

It's not the last link. Your baby will forever link you to him...

She was being silly. It was just a ring, after all. Slowly she tugged at it. After a second's resistance, it came off. It was the first time it had been off her finger since Stephen placed it there six months ago.

Blinking back tears, she told herself she would not cry. She had done enough crying. Today was not a day for crying. Today was a day to be hopeful, a day to look forward into the future, not backward into the past. Like the awakening land around her, she, too, was beginning a new life, and she would begin it without sadness and without thinking of what might have been.

She owed that much to Matt. She owed it to her baby, too. But most of all, she owed it to herself. Resolutely, she palmed the ring, then turned and went back into the house to begin getting ready for her wedding day.

Matt had told Emily he'd pick her up at ten, but he couldn't sleep past six-thirty. By eight, he was showered and dressed and had had his breakfast. He was now drinking his third cup of coffee and wishing the hands of the clock would move faster.

Finally it was nine forty-five, and he could leave. He pulled into Emily's driveway ten minutes later. His heart was beating too fast, and he had the irrational fear that when he rang her doorbell she would tell him she'd changed her mind.

Knowing he was being ridiculous, he told himself to cool it and calmly got out of the car and walked up onto her front porch.

She must have been watching for him, because her door opened before he'd had a chance to ring the bell.

His breath caught when he saw her. She looked so beautiful. The rose lace dress was a perfect counterpoint to her creamy skin and dark hair, which fell in soft waves to her shoulders. Her pregnancy had put a healthy bloom back into her cheeks and added becoming curves to her body. He was filled with a sense of awe. This incredible woman was going to be his wife.

"Hi." Her smile was shy.

"Hi."

There was an uncomfortable silence.

"You...you look beautiful," Matt finally managed. He felt like a gawky schoolboy.

"Thank you." Her gaze was approving as she took in his dark blue pin-striped suit and new white shirt. "You look pretty nice yourself."

He grinned, his unaccustomed nervousness easing. "What can I say? I clean up well."

She chuckled, and suddenly all the awkwardness between them was gone.

"You ready?" he said.

"Yes."

"Where's your bag?" They wouldn't be coming back to San Pedro after the wedding, but driving straight to San Antonio, where Matt had reserved a suite for them at the Hyatt Regency Hotel on the Riverwalk.

"Right here." She pointed to a black soft-side suitcase, which sat just inside the open door.

Matt reached for the bag and waited while she locked the front door. Then, together, they walked to the truck. He opened the tailgate and tossed her suitcase into the back of the Bronco where it joined his own. After helping Emily up into the passenger seat, he walked around and got in beside her. He inserted the key into the ignition, but before turning it he looked at her. Their eyes met. "You okay?" he said.

She nodded.

"You know, on the way here, I thought you might have changed your mind."

"No." She frowned. "*You* haven't changed your mind, have you?"

"Not a chance." He turned the key, and the Bronco sprang to life. "I'm more sure than ever." He put the truck in reverse, but before backing out of the driveway, he met her eyes again. "I don't want you to worry about anything. This is all going to work out."

She nodded again, this time more slowly.

"Because from now on, we're a team."

Now she smiled. "I like that. A team."

He grinned. "And if anybody gives us trouble, look out."

When she laughed, he figured he'd done his job. Minutes later, they were on the highway headed toward Waco.

Emily watched the scenery, which was mostly pastures filled with cattle and an occasional glimpse of a ranch house. She kept her mind as blank as possible, because she wanted no last-minute doubts creeping in.

Her ploy worked. Before she knew it, they were on the outskirts of Waco and Matt was pulling the Bronco into the parking lot of an open-air flower market.

She gave him a quizzical look.

"Every bride needs flowers."

"Oh, Matt, that's sweet, but it's really not necessary."

He paid no attention to her. When she held the bouquet of tiny pink roses and baby's breath in her arms, she had to admit she felt more festive and bridelike. "Thank you, Matt. They're lovely."

He grinned. "Let that be a lesson to you."

"What do you mean?"

"It means I'm always right."

Emily laughed. "I don't think I'll even *attempt* to answer that one." She knew what he was doing, and she appreciated it.

After leaving the flower market, they followed their written directions and, without too much trouble, found the home of the justice of the peace who would marry them.

Justice Davis turned out to be a short, round man with jolly eyes and a jolly wife to match.

"What a lovely couple!" she gushed when she joined her husband in the parlor of their home. "And what a beautiful dress." She beamed at Emily.

Emily couldn't help smiling back. "Thank you, Mrs. Davis."

"And such gorgeous flowers. Well, we must have music, too, don't you think?" Mrs. Davis bustled over to a nearby cabinet. She opened the doors, revealing a CD player. Seconds later, an instrumental with lots of violins played softly in the background. "There now," she said happily, her bright eyes shining with satisfaction, "we're all ready." Taking Matt's arm, she said, "Now, you stand here, and..." She turned to Emily. "You stand right next to him, my dear. You can take his arm if you want to."

Matt smiled down at her, and Emily slipped her hand under his arm. She was glad of the support for her knees felt a bit shaky.

Justice Davis began to read the words of the marriage ceremony.

At first Emily felt curiously detached, as if it were someone else standing there next to Matt. The words flowed over and around her, but didn't really affect her.

Then Justice Davis looked at her and said, "Emily, do you take this man, Matthew, to be your lawful wedded husband, for richer, for poorer, in sickness and in health, till death do you part?"

And just like that, reality hit her.

For richer, for poorer, in sickness and in health, till death do you part...

She swallowed hard. A long, silent moment passed, broken only by the music in the background, and the steady thud of her heartbeat.

Till death do you part...

"Emily?" Matt said.

She blinked. They were all watching her. She could feel the tension in Matt's body as he waited for her response.

She took a deep breath. "I—I do."

She felt rather than heard Matt's sigh of relief.

Justice Davis smiled and turned to Matt. "And do you, Matthew, take this woman, Emily, as your lawful wedded wife, for richer, for poorer, in sickness and in health, till death do you part?"

"I do," Matt said firmly and without hesitation.

Emily felt dazed and slightly unsteady. She tightened her hold on Matt's arm.

"The ring?" Justice Davis prompted.

Gently extricating himself from her grip, Matt reached into his lapel pocket, then took her left hand.

As he slipped her new wedding ring on her finger, Emily thought about the gold band she'd buried at the bottom of her jewelry box only that morning. And then she looked down at the ring Matt had placed on her hand, and the memory vanished as shock reverberated through her. Diamonds, dozens of them, sparkled in the sunlight. She stared at the wide circle of stones, hardly able to believe her eyes. The ring was the most beautiful she'd ever seen. It…it was incredible. She raised her head slowly, her flustered gaze meeting Matt's.

He smiled down at her, and something warm curled deep inside.

"I now pronounce you husband and wife," Justice Davis announced.

Mrs. Davis clapped. "Congratulations!"

"You may now kiss the bride," the justice said.

Emily's heart fluttered as Matt put his arms around her. She lifted her face, and his mouth settled against hers gently. The kiss was over in moments, yet it left her lips tingling and her heart beating faster, and she found she couldn't quite meet Matt's eyes.

Mrs. Davis insisted they stay and have a glass of punch and some cookies. "It's just a little something I always have for my brides and grooms," she said.

Emily didn't have the heart to say no. And truth to tell, having punch and cookies in the presence of the Davises gave her time to get her emotions under control before she and Matt were alone again.

She felt so strange. So confused. And so different from when she and Stephen were married. Then she'd been giddy with happiness, drunk with love and absolutely certain that from then on life would be wonderful, that nothing bad could ever touch her again.

Now she knew better.

Now she knew that the moment you started feeling too contented was the most dangerous time of all, because your life could change in an instant.

"Let's drink a toast," Mrs. Davis said. She raised her glass of punch.

Matt smiled at Emily, and they raised their glasses.

"To love," Mrs. Davis said. "May you love each other forever just as deeply as you do today."

Emily didn't know where to look. She wondered what Matt was thinking. She sneaked a glance at him as she drank her punch. His expression disconcerted her, because it wasn't what she'd expected. She'd thought he would be smiling, amused by Mrs. Davis and her toast. Instead, his eyes held a different emotion, one she couldn't put a name to. Whatever it was, when he realized she was looking at him, he quickly masked it. Soon after, it was time for them to leave and Emily dismissed the moment from her mind.

They said their goodbyes amidst another flurry of well wishes from Mrs. Davis and her smiling husband, then climbed into the Bronco and headed for San Antonio.

Emily could feel Matt's eyes on her throughout the three-hour drive. She knew he was worried about her and wondering how she was feeling. She wished she could reassure him, but her emotions were still so confused, she really didn't want to talk about them.

Not yet, anyway.

He'd been so sweet all day. The way he'd joked with her this morning, trying to put her at ease. And again during the ceremony.

Remembering the ceremony, she lifted her hand so she could study her ring. She had never owned anything so lovely. It must have cost a fortune. She still couldn't believe Matt had given her such a ring.

Why? she wondered. Why had he felt he needed to? She would have been happy with a plain gold band. Yet the gesture touched her.

"Do you like it?" he said.

Startled, she dropped her hand. "I love it. It's gorgeous."

"I'm glad."

"But I know it was terribly expensive, Matt, and you really didn't have to give me anything like this. I didn't expect it."

He didn't reply for a few seconds. "Don't you know, Emily, that it's just because you don't expect it that makes people want to do things for you?"

After that, they didn't talk. Matt put a tape in the tape deck and they listened to music. Emily was glad. She was beginning to tire. Pregnancy did that to women, she'd discovered.

They arrived in San Antonio a little after three. By the time they got checked into their hotel, it was close to four. By then, the stress of the day combined with her more fragile physical condition had really caught up with her, and she desperately needed to rest.

Matt took one look at her and said, ''Tell you what. Why don't you take a nap, and I'll go exploring? Find us a place to have dinner.''

''That sounds wonderful,'' she said gratefully.

''I'll just hang up a few clothes, then I'll be out of your way.''

Once he was gone, Emily undressed and put on her robe. Then she sank onto the bed and closed her eyes.

Within minutes, she was asleep.

Matt took his time, leisurely strolling along the Riverwalk. Each time he came to a restaurant, he stopped and studied the menu so that he'd have suggestions for their dinner later.

When he returned to their suite ninety minutes later, Emily was asleep on the king-size bed. She didn't stir as he came in, not even when he sat on the side of the bed.

In sleep, all the worries of the past week were erased from her face. She looked peaceful and free of care. She wore a pale blue robe, and her feet were bare. She had small feet with high arches, and her toenails were short and painted a light pink. For some reason, they made her look younger and more defenseless.

Tenderness and a need to protect her nearly overwhelmed him. She'd been through so much in her short life, lost so much, had to deal with so much pain. From now on, he wanted things to be different for her. He wanted to take every burden and carry it for her. Make her life easy and filled with only good things. Above all, he vowed he would never let anyone hurt her again.

Because he couldn't help himself, he reached out and gently touched her hip, letting his hand linger against her warmth for a few seconds. She sighed, and he reluctantly removed his hand. He didn't want to wake her. She needed her sleep.

But Lord, how he wished. He wished he could lie down next to her and fit his body to hers. He wished he could slip his arms around her and touch her.

He wished...

Abruptly, he broke off the thought. *Stop torturing yourself.* It's too soon for that. He knew he would have to be patient. Let their relationship proceed at her pace. That was okay. He could do it. It was enough that she was his wife.

He sat there watching her for a long time.

Chapter Eight

Emily stretched and opened her eyes slowly. For a few seconds, she thought she was at home. Then, in a rush, memory returned.

She was in San Antonio.

With Matt.

This was her wedding day.

She sat up. Looked around the bedroom of their suite. Realized again how beautiful it was—the nicest room she'd ever stayed in. Of course, she thought ruefully, she wasn't exactly a sophisticated traveler. Still, even with her limited knowledge of hotels, she knew Matt had splurged on this suite.

Dear Matt.

It constantly amazed her that a man could be so strong and tough on the outside, and so thoughtful and sensitive on the inside. Although their marriage was more a business arrangement than anything else, he was really trying to make it as nice as possible.

She stretched again. What time was it? Glancing at the bedside clock, she saw it was after six. My goodness! She'd slept nearly two hours. Was Matt still out? Just as she began to wonder when he'd be back, the bedroom door opened, and he walked into the room.

He smiled. "So you're awake."

"Oh, hi. Did you just get back?"

"No, I've been back for a while."

"You have? Why didn't you wake me? I never intended to sleep so long."

"I didn't have the heart. You obviously needed the rest." He walked over to the bed and sat on the corner.

"But look how late it is."

"Doesn't matter. We're not on any schedule."

He looked nice, dressed in a collarless navy blue shirt and tan chinos. It was obvious he'd already had his shower and was dressed for the evening. "So I have time to take a shower before we go to dinner?"

"All the time you want."

Emily took him at his word and allowed herself a leisurely shower. Afterward, she indulged herself with a bottle of body lotion she found mixed in with the guest soaps and shampoo. It smelled heavenly and made her feel pampered as she slowly massaged it into her skin.

After towel-drying her hair, she combed it free of

tangles and carefully made up her face. Normally, she didn't wear much makeup, just a little lipstick and blush and occasionally a touch of eye shadow. Tonight she decided she'd go all out. Foundation, eyeliner, mascara. She even curled her eyelashes.

When she was finished with her makeup, she dried her hair with the hair dryer, then looked over the clothes she'd packed. Along with more casual clothing, she'd brought along two transitional outfits that she hoped would carry her through until her pregnancy really began showing. She decided on the dressier of the two—loose-fitting silky pants and a long tunic top in a deep shade of turquoise. With it she wore the turquoise-and-silver earrings her mother had given her for a long-ago birthday. Perfect, she thought, satisfied that she looked her best.

Finally ready, she walked out into the living room portion of their suite. The balcony door was open, and she could see Matt standing outside.

"Nice, isn't it?" he said when she joined him at the balcony railing.

Ten stories below people strolled along the Riverwalk. Lights twinkled in the trees and mariachi music drifted up from one of the restaurants. A balmy breeze lifted Emily's hair. She sighed with pleasure. "Very nice."

"You look beautiful," he murmured, taking her hand. Then, surprising her, he lifted it and gently kissed the back. "Mrs. Thompson."

Her pulse quickened the way it had when he'd kissed her earlier—at the conclusion of their wedding ceremony—and when she answered, her voice was a little breathless. "Th-thank you." Her gaze shied away in confusion as he released her hand.

"Ready to go?"

Still not meeting his eyes, she nodded. "Yes." What was wrong with her? She was being ridiculous. It wasn't as if Matt had given her a passionate kiss or anything. And yet there was something very affecting about the way he'd kissed her hand and said *Mrs. Thompson.*

They walked out of the suite and down the hall to the elevator. He pushed the button. As they waited for the car, Emily surreptitiously studied Matt. She'd always thought of him as attractive, in a quiet, rugged kind of way, but now she realized he was sexy, too.

Very sexy.

How was it that she'd never noticed before? The realization disconcerted her. The fact that she'd noticed *now* disconcerted her even more.

She was glad when the elevator arrived and there were several other people already in it. Now there was something else to look at. Something else to think about. Even so, she was keenly aware of Matt standing behind her as they rode to the lobby level. His cologne, something woodsy and masculine, filled her senses.

When they reached the bottom level, he put his hand at the small of her back to gently guide her out of the car and through the crowded hotel lobby. Through the thin silk, his hand felt warm and strong, and again her pulse picked up speed. Once they were outside, he removed his hand, and she wasn't sure if she was disappointed or relieved.

"You hungry?"

"Starved," she admitted.

"Good. Me, too. I checked out some of the restaurants when I was out earlier."

"Did you find anything you liked?"

"Yeah, there were several that looked good. A couple of Mexican ones, a seafood one and there's also an Italian place that had a great-looking menu."

"So what do you think?"

He grinned. "I was going to leave it up to you."

"In that case, I vote for Italian."

"Italian it is."

The restaurant had been a good choice, Emily decided later, sitting back and sighing, replete with Caesar salad, chicken piccata and Italian cream cake with raspberry sauce. "That was wonderful."

"I'm glad you enjoyed it."

"I'm embarrassed that I ate so much, though."

He smiled affectionately. "I like a gal with a healthy appetite. Besides, you're pregnant."

"Yes, but Dr. Talbot warned me about gaining too much weight. He says it makes delivery more difficult if you do."

"So you'll watch when we get back home. This is our honeymoon. You deserve to enjoy it."

This is our honeymoon. You deserve to enjoy it.

Except for those few moments of awkwardness at the hotel, Emily *had* been enjoying herself, but now that the evening was drawing to a close, she was beginning to feel anxious.

Soon it would be time to go back. And then what? The problem was, she didn't know what Matt expected of her. Would he want to make love tonight?

I can't. I just can't. She realized she'd been lying to herself, thinking she could be a real wife to Matt. *It's too soon.*

She should have talked to Matt about this. She should have made sure they had some kind of understanding. That he realized it would take some time before she would be ready for sexual intimacy.

But she hadn't. And now she didn't know what to do or what he was thinking.

She dawdled over her coffee, postponing the moment when they would have to leave. But finally she could stall no longer, and Matt beckoned the waiter to bring the bill.

Once they were outside the restaurant, Matt said, "Want to walk along the river for a while before we go back?"

"Oh," Emily said, trying not to sound too relieved, "that would be nice." She forced a lighthearted laugh. "Walk off some of those calories."

He smiled and tucked her hand under his arm, turning in the opposite direction from their hotel.

They strolled slowly. There were a lot of other people doing the same thing, because it was a beautiful night. Colorful lanterns bobbed overhead, their lights reflected on the dark surface of the water. Birds flitted through the trees lining the walkway, and gondolas filled with laughing tourists glided past.

Ordinarily Emily would have enjoyed the walk, but tonight wasn't ordinary. Tonight was her wedding night, and she couldn't escape the troubling question of whether Matt would expect to make love to her when they got back to the hotel.

So what will you do if he wants to? She would never refuse him, of course. He was her husband, and she would honor her commitment to him, but if they *did* make love tonight, she was bound to disappoint him.

And Matt didn't deserve that. He was too fine a man, and he had been too good to her. He deserved a wholehearted and enthusiastic response, and she knew she was incapable of giving that to him right now.

Stealing a glance at him, she wondered if she dared say what she was thinking. She dismissed the thought as soon as it formed. No, she couldn't. She would be too embarrassed. Besides, it was presumptuous. Maybe he wasn't thinking along those lines at all. Still, she worried and wished they could just stay out here, walking companionably along the Riverwalk, forever.

Too soon, though, it was time to turn back. Emily's anxiety escalated with every step they took. The closer they got to the hotel, the more nervous she became. And then they were standing outside the door to their suite and Matt was unlocking it.

He stepped back to let her precede him. As Emily

walked in, she whispered a silent prayer. *Please, God, help me be a good wife to Matt.* Taking a deep breath, she turned to face him. The moment of truth had come.

He smiled down at her, his eyes warm and kind. "Tired?"

She nodded. "A little."

"It's been a big day."

"Yes."

"Tell you what. You go on and get ready for bed. I'll go sit out on the balcony for a while. Give you some privacy."

"A-all right."

"And, Emily?"

"Yes?"

"Don't worry." He touched her cheek, caressing it gently. "I know it's too soon."

Relief flooded her. He understood. Oh, thank God, he understood.

She placed her hand over his and gazed up into his eyes. "Thank you, Matt. I don't know what I ever did to deserve you."

After Emily disappeared into the bedroom, Matt walked out to the balcony. He stood at the railing and stared unseeingly at the scene below. It had been hard to say what he had, because he wanted nothing more than to go inside and make love to Emily tonight. He couldn't, though. He knew her so well, and it was obvious to him that she was worried earlier—both during dinner and afterward. And it hadn't been hard to figure out exactly what it was that worried her.

She was nervous about what would happen when they got back to the hotel. More specifically, what would happen when they went to bed.

I've waited this long. I can wait until she's ready, he told himself, because as much as he loved her and wanted her, he didn't want her out of a sense of obligation. He wanted her to want him, too. Otherwise, being with her would be the hollowest of victories.

So no matter how long it took—days, weeks, months—he would wait.

He let a half hour go by before joining her in the bedroom. Wearing a lacy pink nightgown, she was already in bed and, if anything, looked even lovelier than she'd looked earlier.

To spare her any embarrassment, he undressed in the bathroom. Normally he slept in the nude, but he'd brought pajama bottoms along to wear tonight. After putting them on and brushing his teeth, he walked out into the bedroom.

While he'd been in the bathroom, she'd turned off the bedside light, and now the room was illuminated only by the moonlight spilling in through the window. Slipping into bed beside her, Matt tried not to think about how her nightgown clung to her softly rounded breasts or how warm she would be if he put his arms around her and pulled her close. He tried not to imagine how her body would feel fitted up next to his, nor how her skin would feel if he stroked it. But no matter how he tried, he couldn't seem to help himself. The images refused to go away.

She was so close, only inches away. He could still faintly smell the flowery fragrance she'd worn earlier. He ached, he wanted her so badly.

Stop torturing yourself. Just lean over and kiss her cheek and tell her good-night.

It was all he could do to follow his orders. But somehow he did. Somehow he raised himself up and gently kissed her cheek. Somehow he murmured, "Good night, Emily," and turned over on his side.

He lay awake a long time, listening to her quiet breathing and struggling to tamp down his tumultuous emotions. His last thought before falling asleep was that being with Emily, yet not being with her in all the ways he wanted to be, might be tougher than he'd believed.

It took Emily a long time to fall asleep. She was acutely conscious of Matt beside her and, although she didn't want to, she kept remembering another wedding night and how different it had been. Then she'd turned to her husband eagerly and passionately. Then she'd welcomed his lovemaking, reveled in it.

She kept shifting her eyes to Matt. Looking at his broad back. Listening to his breathing. She knew he wasn't asleep.

What was he thinking? Was he sorry he married her? In some ways, she wished he *had* wanted to make love to her tonight. Maybe that would have been best. Then the awkwardness would be behind them.

She could hardly admit it to herself, but the physical sharing would have been comforting. No, she was not *in* love with Matt, but she did care for him—very much. For a moment, she considered touching his back, letting him know she would be willing. But she couldn't drum up enough courage; her feelings were too confused—she felt vulnerable and uncertain.

No, it was best this way. To be the kind of wife Matt deserved, she needed time, and Matt realized it. She sighed and turned on her side, away from him. Determinedly, she closed her eyes.

And eventually she fell asleep, too.

On Sunday, Matt ordered a room service breakfast. They ate the fresh fruit and waffles and crisp bacon seated outside on their balcony, with the sun warming their skin, and the food warming their insides.

After breakfast, they took their respective showers and dressed in casual clothes: Emily in white stirrup pants, white sneakers and a red-and-white tunic-style T-shirt, her hair pulled back with a red headband; Matt in jeans, a yellow knit shirt and worn Adidas.

They walked along the Riverwalk again, stopping periodically to gaze into shop windows. When the stores opened at noon, Matt insisted on going back to the ones where Emily had oohed and aahed over the displays.

When they were finished shopping, she owned a new watch, a brass kaleidoscope, silver earrings in the shape of stars, a tiny gold locket on a delicate chain and a gorgeous pale green cashmere baby blanket.

"This is too much, Matt," she protested once.

"It gives me pleasure to do things for you, Emily. Don't you know that by now?"

His answer touched her deeply, and once again she asked God to help her be worthy of Matt, and prayed that she could make him a good wife.

Later that afternoon, they toured the Alamo—which Emily enjoyed immensely—then they headed back to their suite, where Emily took a short nap while Matt sat out on the balcony and read the Clive Cussler novel he'd brought along.

That night, dressed up again, they ate dinner at the hotel, then drove to a club recommended by the concierge, where they listened to wonderful blues music until Emily's eyelids began to droop and Matt decided it was time "for all pregnant women to be in bed."

Once again, he simply kissed Emily on the cheek and nothing more.

On Monday, they got up early and ate breakfast in the hotel restaurant. Afterward, they headed for the *mercado,* the Mexican market, where they bought straw hats and colorful pottery and a beaten silver-and-turquoise bracelet for Emily.

"To match your earrings," Matt said.

Emily couldn't believe he'd noticed. Stephen never would have. Immediately she felt guilty for the thought, and yet why should she? It was the truth.

In the afternoon, she and Matt swam in the hotel's heated indoor pool, and later they took in an early movie, after which they had dinner at one of the Mexican restaurants.

While waiting for their flan, Matt said, ''Well, tomorrow we go home.''

''I know,'' Emily said regretfully. She hated to see the honeymoon end. The past two days had been wonderful. Matt had been wonderful, she thought fondly. Once she'd realized he wouldn't rush her into sexual intimacy, she had been able to relax and enjoy herself.

In fact, she'd felt guilty about being so happy, when Stephen had been dead such a short time. Yet, in her heart, she knew Stephen wouldn't have minded. He'd had his faults, just like anyone else, but selfishness was not one of them. He wouldn't want her to grieve or to spend the rest of her life alone.

And he had thought the world of Matt. So each time guilt threatened, she'd dismissed it from her mind and allowed herself to enjoy being pampered and spoiled and treated like a princess.

But the honeymoon had to end, and Emily and Matt had to go back to San Pedro…and reality in the form of Cornelia Pierce.

What would Cornelia do when she found out they were married? Emily was uncertain about many things, but of one thing she was completely sure. Whatever reaction Cornelia had concerning Emily's marriage to Matt, it would not be pleasant.

After stewing for more than a week, Cornelia awoke on Tuesday morning determined to try one last time to talk some sense into Emily. So after morning chores were over, she took a quick shower, changed into clean clothes and drove into town.

On the way, she had decided what she would say. Even though it galled her, she knew she would have to curb her inclination to give orders. Obviously that tactic wouldn't work with Stephen's wife. Instead, she would appeal to Emily's better nature—if the woman *had* one—and explain how much it would have meant to Stephen to have his child raised at Pierce Ranch. Yes, that was the tack to take. And in the process, she could emphasize not only all the advantages there would be for the child, but how much easier life would be for Emily.

Shortly before ten, she pulled into the parking area outside the small frame building housing Matt Thompson's Flying Service. She told herself to be pleasant if it killed her, and opened the door.

But it wasn't Emily who looked up from behind the desk. It was Matt's sister, Pam Morland. Cornelia frowned. At one time, she had liked Pam, but that was before she and her husband had opposed Cornelia over a proposed change in zoning restrictions. They hadn't managed to sway the county commissioner to their way of thinking, but it wasn't for lack of trying. Cornelia had never forgotten their opposition, and she never would.

"Hello, Mrs. Pierce." Pam's smile was polite, her eyes guarded. "What brings you into town this morning?"

"I came to see Emily," Cornelia said stiffly. "Please tell her I'm here."

"I'm sorry, but that's not possible," Pam said.

"And why is that?" Cornelia demanded.

"She's out of town."

"Out of town? What do you mean, *out of town?*" What was wrong with the woman? She was pregnant with Cornelia's grandchild. She had no business gallivanting around. "Where did she go?"

Pam shrugged. "I don't think Emily's whereabouts are any of your business."

Cornelia's eyes narrowed. "Now see here, Pamela Morland, don't you give me any of your smart mouth. If Emily's not here, you just march your butt into your brother's office and tell him I want to see him! Now!" Her voice shook, she was so angry. The unbelievable impertinence of the woman! How dare she speak to Cornelia in that snotty tone.

"My brother is out of town, too," Pam said with fake sweetness.

"Oh, really?"

"Yes, really."

"I knew it! They're together. I knew that girl had no class the first time I laid eyes on—"

"Excuse me," Pam interrupted. "I think you'd better be careful what you say about my sister-in-law."

"S-sister-in-law!" Cornelia sputtered, shock reverberating through her.

Pam's smile was triumphant. "Yes. You see, it is my great pleasure to inform you, Mrs. Pierce, that my brother and Emily were married on Saturday and are even now on their honeymoon.''

Cornelia stared at her. She couldn't have heard correctly. "Married?"

"Yes, married.''

Cornelia wanted nothing so much as to slap that smug, self-satisfied look off Pam Morland's face. She clenched her fists and willed herself to calm down, even as she absorbed the knowledge that Emily would not be moving out to the ranch. That she had married Matt Thompson when Stephen had only been dead a little over two months. That Stephen's child would be living under Matt Thompson's roof...and under Matt Thompson's influence. "I don't believe you," she finally retorted.

"Suit yourself." Pam turned her attention back to her computer, acting as if Cornelia were no longer there. She began to type.

Cornelia glared at her. She had never felt so impotent. She wanted to scream at Pam, tell her exactly what she thought of her *and* her brother *and* her new sister-in-law, but she knew she'd only look foolish if she did. After a long, tense moment passed, she finally said, in the coldest possible voice, "You will be sorry that you have chosen to speak to me in this way, Mrs. Morland, and your brother and his *wife* will be sorry for their actions, too. You can tell them for me that, despite what they might think, their marriage changes nothing. Nothing. Do you understand?''

Pam looked up. "I understand perfectly.''

Because she couldn't think of a last, cutting remark, Cornelia contented herself with giving Pam one last malevolent look, then swung on her heel and left.

She fumed all the way home.

If that baby really was Stephen's, there was no way she would permit Matt Thompson to raise him. No way. And if Emily and Matt thought otherwise, they thought wrong.

I'll hire the best lawyers in the state of Texas. No matter how long it takes, or what I have to do to accomplish it, that child will be raised at Pierce Ranch.

Suddenly she felt calmer. Why had she gotten so upset? The battle was far from over. In fact, it was only just beginning. She had a few trump cards of her own to play, and if a couple of nobodies like Emily and Matt Thompson thought they had bested her, they were about to learn differently.

Chapter Nine

They didn't check out of their hotel until nearly noon on Tuesday.

"Oh, Matt, you shouldn't have let me sleep so late!" Emily said, dismayed when she realized it was already after nine.

"You looked so peaceful sleeping, I didn't have the heart to wake you. Besides, there's no hurry. I thought it would be nice to have one last leisurely breakfast before we pack up and head on out."

"That *does* sound nice."

Emily had been on so few pleasure trips in her life that she liked the idea of prolonging this one, especially now that she no longer had to worry about the physical part of her marriage.

Well, that wasn't *quite* true. One of these days Matt

would certainly expect her to be his wife in all senses of the word...and Emily wanted to be... Of course, she did...because anything less would be terribly unfair to him.

But still, she was enormously grateful that Matt had been sensitive to her fragile emotional state and had given her this wonderfully relaxing and peaceful hiatus—an interlude she'd sorely needed.

Matt was the perfect companion, she reflected as she showered and prepared herself for the day. The thought gave her a twinge, as if she were being disloyal to Stephen, but how could that be? They were completely different men who had different attitudes and approaches to life.

With Stephen, there was always an air of excitement surrounding whatever they were doing. Sometimes, in fact, there had been *too* much excitement for Emily's taste—although she'd always quickly banished the thought—but Stephen wasn't interested in quiet pursuits. She couldn't imagine him being contented with leisurely strolls along the Riverwalk and quiet dinners and early nights such as she'd had with Matt. Stephen always had to be doing something, going somewhere. Even at home, he was a night owl, preferring to stay up late and sleep late in the morning, whereas Emily liked going to bed early and rising early.

"What's the appeal about morning?" Stephen had groused once when she'd slipped out of bed before six on a weekend morning. "In my opinion, not having to get up with the chickens is the best thing about *not* living on the ranch.''

"Mornings are so lovely and peaceful," Emily said. "So quiet. You can *think* in the morning."

She remembered how he'd put his arms around her and lured her back into bed. "Who wants to think?" he said, nuzzling her ear. "Doing is much more fun than thinking."

Emily laughed. "We can't *always* be having fun."

"Why not? If more people concentrated on having fun and less on work, the world would be a much better place. Take my mother, for instance. All she thinks about is work." He rolled his eyes. "To her, the ranch is everything."

"But, Stephen, people *have* to work. Besides, I like working. I like knowing I'm doing a good job, don't you?"

"Emily, sweetness, you're so serious about everything. Frankly, I think work is boring. If I never had to work again, I'd be happy."

Afterward, she told herself Stephen didn't really mean what he'd said. He might *think* he would be happy playing forever, but that was because he hadn't yet found his niche. When he did, he would discover that there was great satisfaction in meaningful work. Yes, she'd assured herself, things would change, his *attitude* would change, when he had a job he loved. She'd ignored the thread of disquiet his comments had produced. Ignored the disturbing suspicion that maybe his mother was right. That maybe Emily and

Stephen, despite the tremendous physical attraction between them, were totally mismatched people.

Later, as she and Matt were in the Bronco on their way back to San Pedro, she found herself thinking once more of the differences between Matt and Stephen.

"Matt," she said, "if you won the lottery, would you quit working?"

He chuckled, giving her a sidelong glance. "What made you think of that?"

"I don't know."

"Considering I don't play the lottery, it would be pretty hard for me to win."

"But if you *did*..."

"If I did, no, I probably wouldn't quit working."

"Because?"

"Because I'd be bored if I didn't have work to do."

"But you like to read and work in the yard and build things. Wouldn't that be enough?"

"No, I don't think so. I think people need a purpose in life. Besides, I love what I do. Half the time, it's more fun than work." He smiled. "What about you? If, while you were in Houston studying bookkeeping, you'd won the lottery, would you have dropped out of school and just had fun the rest of your life?"

Emily shook her head. "No. I feel the way you do. I like having work to do."

They both fell silent after that, but Emily continued to think about what he had said and how, even though she never would have imagined it to be true—and even now her heart wanted to deny it even as her head refused to let go of the thought—Matt was much more suited to be her husband than Stephen had ever been.

They pulled into the driveway of Matt's house in the early afternoon. Emily had been there before, several times, and he knew she liked the house, but there was a world of difference between being there as a guest and coming there as his wife. He figured the next few minutes would be awkward, and he was determined to put her at ease.

He watched her covertly as they unloaded the car and she seemed okay, even giving him a little smile when their eyes met.

"Tired?" he said.

She shook her head. "Stiff, that's all."

He unlocked the back door, and she preceded him into the kitchen. Once inside, she paused.

He inclined his head. "Through there," he said, gesturing toward the hallway. "We might as well take this stuff into the bedroom."

"You lead, I'll follow," she said, smiling, but there was an uncertainty in her expression that tugged at his heart. He knew he had to do or say something to dispel the awkwardness or it would only get worse.

She stepped aside as he hefted their bags and headed for the master bedroom, which faced the front of the house. Once they reached their destination, he dropped the bags on the floor and turned to face her.

For one unguarded moment, her eyes were clouded over with sadness, and he knew she was remembering earlier, happier days. Right then, he hated Stephen Pierce, not only for making her sad but for intruding on a day when Matt wanted Emily to be thinking only of him. Only of them and their future together.

He reached for her hand. "Emily."

She swallowed. Her attempt at a cheerful smile fell short, but he could see how she was struggling to show him she was okay. Suddenly he was ashamed of himself. Of course she was sad. What was he thinking? It was only a little over two months since she'd lost her husband. And just because she'd agreed to marry *him* didn't mean she could just turn off her feelings or make them go away.

"Emily," he said again, "listen, it's okay if you feel sad. I understand."

She bit her bottom lip. Nodded. Made a valiant attempt to smile again, but couldn't. "I'm sorry, Matt. I know you're probably sick of me."

"No. No, I'm not." He was still holding her hand, and he squeezed it. "I told you. I understand. It took me *years* to get over losing Joan and Laurie. The way you're feeling...it's normal."

She took a long, shaky breath. Met his eyes. "I promise you, though, it won't always be like this. I *will* get over it. It was just that...well, coming here...it just reminded me of when...Stephen and I came back from our honeymoon. I—I'm sorry. It... it's so ungrateful of me...after all you've done."

Because he loved her so much, and because he was

only human, he pulled her into his arms, tucking her head under his chin. He could feel the tremors in her body, and knew she was close to tears. "I don't want you to talk like that anymore," he said fiercely. "I haven't *done* anything. I wanted to marry you, and I knew what I was getting myself into. And I don't want you apologizing, either. I wouldn't think much of you if you *weren't* still grieving for Stephen."

After a long moment, she pulled back a little and looked up at him. Tears shimmered. "Thanks, Matt. It won't always be like this. I promise."

"I know."

"Now," she said, forcing a brightness into her voice he knew she didn't feel. "Why don't you show me where you keep everything, and I'll get us unpacked?"

There was only one other bad moment, and this time it was Matt who experienced it. It happened as he was showing Emily the bedroom wing and they reached the room that had been Laurie's. It was still painted pink and the windows still had the lavender-and-pink striped curtains Joan had made, even though Matt had long since given to charity the white four-poster bed and matching dresser, the dollhouse and the Barbies, the dresses and the shoes. Now the room contained a daybed and a small TV set and nothing much else. Matt never entered it if he could help it, but he'd honestly thought the heartache was behind him.

"I thought this would be the baby's room." He stood aside to let Emily walk in ahead of him, and that was when the memory hit him, and, with it, a raw blast of pain that found him completely unprepared.

Laurie had been almost three, and one night she'd disappeared into her room while he and Joan were watching the six o'clock news.

After a while Joan looked at him and said, "She's awfully quiet in there."

He'd gotten up. "I'll go check on her."

He'd walked down the hall and stopped at her open doorway. What he saw made him smile. Laurie, still round with baby fat, was standing in front of her mirrored closet. She'd pulled up her T-shirt and pushed down her shorts so that her belly button was exposed. She was poking at it in great curiosity.

"Hey, sunshine," he said. "Whatcha doin'?"

She looked up, her blue eyes narrowed in deep thought. "Lookin' for my bee button."

His smile got wider. "Bee button" was the term Joan always used for belly button, because Ls were hard for little kids to say. "Didn't you find it?" he asked seriously.

She shook her head in perplexity. "No."

"But, honey, it's right there. You were touching your bee button."

"No, I wasn't, Daddy. That's not a *button!* Dis is a button!" And she'd opened the closet door and shown him a button on one of her dresses.

Matt, trying not to laugh, sat down on her bed and pulled her onto his lap and tried to explain how and why her belly button had gotten its name.

Remembering how warm and sweet she'd felt and how much he'd loved her, Matt's throat filled, and he had to excuse himself and leave Emily to inspect the room on her own. He escaped to the master bath and closed the door behind him until he could get his emotions under control. Emily was feeling shaky enough right now. She didn't need his problems to deal with, too. By the time he rejoined her, he was in control again, and the rest of the day passed without incident.

Cornelia's spies must have called her the moment they saw Matt's Bronco enter the city limits of San Pedro, because Emily and Matt hadn't been in the office for more than thirty minutes on Wednesday morning when Cornelia's pickup truck pulled into the parking lot.

"Here comes trouble," Matt muttered from the doorway.

Emily's heart beat a little faster, making her angry with herself. Why did she let Cornelia affect her this way? The woman had no power over her. As she watched, the driver-side door of the pickup opened, and Cornelia stepped down.

Emily made herself smile, and as the outer door opened and Cornelia walked in, she managed to say without a tremor, "Hello, Mrs. Pierce."

Cornelia glared at her. "Have you no shame?"

Emily blinked.

"Just what is it she's supposed to be ashamed of?" Matt said coldly.

Cornelia ignored him, her gaze remaining fixed upon Emily. "It's disgusting, that's what it is. My son is barely cold in his grave, and you've already replaced him in your bed. If you had any decency at all, you'd observe a proper mourning period. Why, you've made Stephen look like a fool for ever marrying you in the first place!"

The words caused Emily to flinch. Although she knew she'd done nothing wrong, she also knew Cornelia's attitude would be shared by many in San Pedro.

Matt walked forward, laying a protective hand on Emily's shoulder. "The only person here who looks like a fool is you, Cornelia. Emily has done nothing wrong."

Cornelia finally turned her icy gaze his way. "You stay out of this. This is between my son's widow and me."

"Since Emily is now my wife, anything that concerns her concerns me."

"It's okay, Matt," Emily said, finally finding her voice.

"It's *not* okay," he said tightly.

"I just want you to know," Cornelia said, once more ignoring Matt, "that this *contemptible* behavior of yours will not be tolerated. Nor will it go unanswered."

Then, not waiting for a reply, she stalked out. Seconds later, they heard the angry squeal of her tires across the tarmac.

Emily's heart was still pounding.

"Don't pay any attention to her," Matt said.

Emily closed her eyes. Not pay attention? How could she help but? Cornelia wasn't the sort to be ignored. She made her presence felt no matter where she was or who she was with.

"She can't do anything," Matt continued.

Emily looked at him. "I know you're trying to make me feel better, but I can't help it. She frightens me, especially when she's this angry." Instinctively she touched her stomach. "And she's got so many influential friends. You know that, Matt."

"Emily..." Matt drew her to her feet. Hands on her shoulders, he looked deeply into her eyes. "I don't care how many influential friends Cornelia has. She can't do anything. It's going to be okay. I promise."

"I hope you're right." All Emily's newfound tranquility had vanished with Cornelia's vitriol and threats.

Slowly Matt gathered her close. And after a second or two of initial resistance, Emily put her arms around his waist and allowed herself to take comfort from the warmth and strength of his arms.

A few moments later, the phone rang, and Matt released her to allow her to answer it, but he didn't go back to his office. He waited until she was finished with the call, then said, "You okay now?"

Emily nodded.

"You sure?"

"Yes," she said, sighing. "But you know, Matt, I'm sure Stephen's mother isn't the only one who feels that way. I can just hear the town gossips when they find out about us. They'll be saying awful things.''

Matt's jaw clenched. ''Anyone who says a word about you is going to have to answer to me.''

Emily looked away. ''Oh, Matt...''

He lifted her chin, forcing her to look up at him. ''Listen to me, Emily. You've done nothing wrong. *We've* done nothing wrong. And the people who count will know that. Now I want you to promise me you'll put this whole thing out of your mind and just let me take care of it, okay?''

After a moment, she sighed again. ''Okay.''

''No, Cornelia,'' Walker Nesbitt said with barely disguised impatience. ''There is *nothing* you can do about it. Emily is free to marry anyone she wants.''

''But that child she's carrying is *Stephen's* child.''

''I'm aware of that.''

''I do not want Stephen's child raised by Matt Thompson!'' She bit off each word angrily as she paced the width of his office and back.

''It doesn't matter what you want,'' Walker said with a sigh. He rubbed his forehead. He had the beginnings of a doozy of a headache. ''Like it or not, you're not the mother. Emily is.''

She stopped in front of his desk and banged her fist down, causing the framed picture of his grandchildren to fall over. ''But I'm the grandmother! Don't I have any rights?''

Walker shook his head and picked up the picture,

carefully putting it back in its rightful place. "Yes, under the Family Code of Texas, you will have visitation rights. But if you cannot reach an amiable agreement with Emily, the courts will have to decide how often and under what circumstances you may see him or her."

"I don't want to just *see* the child. I want to make sure the child is raised the way a Pierce should be raised. And that means on the ranch. Learning about its heritage. *Not* in Matt Thompson's house where its mind will probably be poisoned against me."

"Cornelia…"

"Don't you *Cornelia* me! I don't want to hear your platitudes and excuses and namby-pamby stuff about Texas law. I want you to tell me just how you plan to solve this problem." With a huff, she sat in one of the chairs flanking his desk and folded her arms.

Walker sighed. For someone as smart as she was, Cornelia Pierce could be totally unreasonable. Still, she was one of his most influential clients, and he couldn't afford to antagonize her. Prudently, he decided to temper the truth with a large dose of tact. "All right, let's talk about this. But first of all, let's get something straight. It was a mistake for you to go over to Matt's office."

"Excuse me?" she bristled, sitting up.

He held up his hand. "But a *natural* mistake. I probably would have done the same thing myself."

"Well…" Mollified for the moment, she settled back into the chair.

"Still, it doesn't pay to tip your hand. You know that."

She grimaced, her nod reluctant.

"But that's over and done with, so let's forget about it. What we need to do now is plan our strategy for after the baby is born. Okay, let's examine your options. The first would be to swallow your pride, apologize to Emily and Matt and try to get on their good side."

"Never."

Walker stifled the urge to sigh again. He should have known she would not take the easy way. Cornelia never took the easy way. "In that case, your only other option is to try to prove that Emily is an unfit mother. That's the one thing that might sway the court into looking favorably upon you as an alternate custodian of the child. But I warn you, Cornelia, it won't be easy. In fact, it may be impossible."

She mulled that information over for a while. Then, nodding, she said, "I've never let the word *impossible* stop me before, Walker. And I don't intend to let it stop me now."

The next few days were so busy, Emily had little time to dwell on Cornelia or her threats. And by the time she and Matt had finished packing up her belongings and moving the furniture she wanted to keep and disposing of the things she didn't want and putting her house up for sale, some of Emily's anxiety had faded, because nothing had happened. Even the gossip Emily had anticipated hadn't materialized, probably because Matt was so well thought of in town.

Still, Emily knew Cornelia was not the kind to make empty threats. But when two weeks passed with no further contact from Stephen's mother, Emily finally began to relax.

And at the end of a month, she decided Matt was right when he'd said he thought Cornelia had finally realized that right now she had no other course of action but acceptance of their marriage.

"I don't think we'll hear from her again until after the baby's born," he added.

With the threat of any immediate action by Cornelia removed, Emily settled into her new life as Matt's wife with relative ease and only an occasional twinge of sadness over the past. Matt was easy to live with, his habits and likes so similar to hers, that their days fell into a comfortable pattern.

They were both early risers, and he always set the alarm for six, but most mornings they would be awake before then. He'd go out into the kitchen and put the coffee on, giving Emily first crack at the master bathroom. She would take a quick shower, then head for the kitchen where she'd prepare breakfast while Matt showered.

By six-thirty, six forty-five at the latest, they would be eating breakfast, and by seven-thirty the kitchen would be cleaned up, the bed would be made, Lorelei's food dish would be filled, a packet of chicken or something would be set out on the drainboard to thaw and they would be ready to leave for the office.

"We're a good team," he commented one day toward the end of May, when they'd been married nearly two months.

"Yes, we are," Emily agreed, smiling.

He'd looked at her thoughtfully for a long moment. "You're happy, aren't you, Emily?"

"Why, yes," she said in some surprise. "I believe I am." She realized that days would now go by without her thinking of Stephen.

Others noticed the change in her, too.

One day when Emily and Nell were having lunch together, Nell said, "Emily, being married to Matt agrees with you."

"I know." She smiled. "He's a really great guy."

Nell nodded, playing with her napkin. "You know, I've been wondering about something for the longest time."

"What?"

Nell hesitated, an odd expression on her face.

"What?"

"Why did you marry Stephen?"

Emily had been about to take a bite of her egg salad sandwich, but at Nell's question, she lowered it to her plate and gave her friend a quizzical smile. "Because I loved him."

Nell nodded.

"I don't understand why you'd even ask that question."

"Well, it's just that you and Matt seem so perfectly suited to each other, and you seem so relaxed and contented since you've married him. Stephen, well, he never seemed your type.'' Nell's eyes met hers. ''If you want to know the truth, I never thought your marriage to Stephen would last.''

''Nell!'' Emily said, shocked.

Nell shrugged. ''I'm sorry, but it's the truth. Let's face it, Emily, Stephen was handsome and charming and everyone liked him, but he was immature. I mean, think about it. He dropped out of college—the rumor was that he *flunked* out of college—and ever since, he spent most of his time doing things like racing cars or skydiving or skiing, all the while spending his mother's money. Of course, she's always been *totally* blind where he was concerned. You know, her expectations regarding him and how he was bound to disappoint her were one of the favorite topics of conversation among the local gossips.''

''Nell,'' Emily said again.

''C'mon, Emily, surely you realized he had a very different approach to life than you did. Honey, I know you loved him. Shoot, Stephen was easy to love. But living with him for a lifetime...that's a whole other ball game. I figured you would've outgrown him by the time you were thirty-five, maybe sooner.''

That afternoon and evening, Emily could think of little else but the things Nell had said. Finally, reluctantly, and again with that old unwelcome feeling of disloyalty, Emily was forced to concede that Nell just might be more right than Emily cared to admit.

Why *had* she married him? She, who had always been so sensible, so levelheaded, so hardworking?

She, who had never been impulsive, who always thought out everything carefully before taking action?

The answer was obvious now.

She'd married him because he made her feel young and carefree and beautiful—all the things she'd never had the luxury of being.

It saddened her to think their marriage might not have lasted. Yet she was too honest not to acknowledge the possibility, especially now, when she was married to someone who was the embodiment of maturity and strength.

More and more, as June turned into July, and July into August, Emily realized how lucky she was to have Matt. Everyone admired and respected him. And his family adored him. They spent a lot of time with Pam and Ben and the kids, and Emily watched how Matt related to them, and they to him.

He will be a wonderful father, she thought, just as he was a wonderful brother to Pam and uncle to the boys. She heard the fondness and love in his voice when he spoke of his parents and their marriage, and as he opened up and talked about his own marriage and the child he lost, she realized he had endured great pain and was a better person in spite of it.

His thoughtfulness constantly amazed her. As her pregnancy advanced, her back began to ache and her feet began to swell. Every night, he gave her a foot massage and insisted she sit with her feet propped up while he fixed their dinner. When she said she felt guilty letting him do all the work, he said he'd get her back after the baby was born, not to worry.

She couldn't help smiling.

For her twenty-ninth birthday at the end of August, he secretly plotted with Nell to throw a little surprise party for her.

Emily knew, if she lived to be a hundred, she would never forget the way it felt to walk into Pam's house and hear a dozen or so of their friends shout, "Happy birthday!"

Tears welled into her eyes, and she nearly broke down. She had never had a birthday party. When she was little, there was never any money. And when she got older, her mother was too sick.

"Hey," Matt said, putting his arm around her shoulders and giving her a hug. "Why the tears? I thought you'd be pleased."

"Oh, Matt," she said, looking up at him, "I *am*. No one has ever done anything this nice for me before."

"Ah, Emily," he murmured, kissing the side of her forehead.

In that moment, Emily wished they had the kind of relationship where she could throw her arms around him and kiss him on the mouth. The thought disconcerted her, and she quickly looked away.

But all night, as they ate and sang songs and played games, it kept returning. She kept stealing glances at Matt. She kept thinking about later, when they went home.

I want him to make love to me.

The realization stunned her. When had this happened? When had her feelings for him changed to include physical desire? She thought back over the past months. The changes had been so subtle she had not been aware of them until now.

I'm finally ready to be his wife...in every way.

And tonight, when they got home, she would tell him so.

Her heart beat faster.

Would he be glad? What if he wasn't? What if she wasn't desirable to him right now? At seven months' pregnant, she'd gained eighteen pounds and was so unwieldy. Some men found pregnant women unattractive. What if Matt was one of them? She realized that he very rarely touched her. Even when the baby first started moving, he'd seemed reluctant to feel her stomach.

She swallowed. *I can't take the chance. I can't put him on the spot that way.*

Emily knew Matt. She knew how chivalrous he was. He would never turn her down. But she didn't want him making love to her because he felt it was his duty!

No.

She couldn't do it.

The most she could do was try to show him by her actions that she was ready. But he would have to make the first move.

Chapter Ten

Sometimes Matt wasn't sure how he had survived the past months. Much of the time, it had been agony.

He wanted Emily so much. He ached from wanting her. The desire he had thought he could keep tamped down and controlled had begun to consume him. It was all he thought about. It was even interfering with his ability to work efficiently.

It seemed to reach its zenith on the night of her birthday party. Even at seven months' pregnant, she was the most desirable woman there. The most desirable woman anywhere. He couldn't take his eyes off her: the rosy bloom in her cheeks, her soft, eminently kissable mouth, her dark glowing eyes, the way she couldn't seem to stop smiling.

It made him feel good to know he was responsible

for the contentment and well-being evidenced by every word and gesture. That he had made her happy by giving her the surprise party.

But damn!

Did she have to be *so* happy?

Because it was obvious to him that Emily was perfectly content with the status quo as far as he was concerned. As far as any sexual intimacy between them was concerned.

So underlying the satisfaction of knowing he had accomplished his goal of taking care of her and making her feel safe was a growing feeling of despair, for he was more and more afraid Emily would never want him the way he wanted her.

He couldn't go on this way much longer. One of these days, he was bound to lose control, and he didn't want that to happen. He wanted their first time together to be tender and slow, as satisfying for her as he could make it.

Maybe he should just force the issue. Maybe, when they got home tonight, he should take her in his arms and say, "Emily, I think it's time we became husband and wife in all ways." Not even put it as a question, not even give her any options.

But even as he considered doing just that, he knew he wouldn't. He didn't want Emily that way. He wanted his desire for her to be reciprocated. And obviously it was not. Not yet, anyway.

All right, so he couldn't force her, but he also couldn't keep this up. It was too hard. What was the answer? Although he didn't want to accept it, there really was only one solution to the problem.

Until she made some kind of move in his direction, he was going to have to try to distance himself from her as much as possible, otherwise he would go crazy.

And he would begin tonight.

Emily had her strategy all planned. Instead of the demure cotton nightgown she usually wore to bed, she decided she would put on the pale blue satin one trimmed in lace that Nell had given her as a present right after Emily and Matt were married. Emily had laughed at the time, saying, "Nell, I don't wear things like this!"

Nell smiled. "Well, you should."

So later, while Matt was locking up the house in preparation for the night, Emily took the nightgown out of the drawer where it had lain since that day. She shook it out. It seemed full enough to accommodate her pregnancy. She smiled. It really was beautiful...and with its clingy material and low-cut neckline of delicate lace, it was also very sexy.

She felt very bold. Very daring. And very nervous. She almost put the nightgown back in the drawer. *Don't be a coward!* Okay, she would do it. She would put the nightgown on and get into bed, and when Matt got in beside her, she would move close to him and touch his back.

Surely he would get the message. And if he wanted her, he would put his arms around her and kiss her. The rest would take care of itself.

Emily's heart beat harder as she prepared herself. She brushed her hair until it shone and dabbed cologne behind her ears and between her breasts. And then, just as she was ready to leave the bathroom, Matt knocked on the door. She opened it a crack and smiled at him. "I'll be out in a minute."

"That's okay, take your time," he said, avoiding her gaze. "I just wanted to tell you I'm not very tired, so I think I'll go into the living room and read awhile. You go on to bed, though."

Her heart sank, but she tried not to show her disappointment, even though he still hadn't met her eyes. "Oh. All right." As he turned to go, she said, "Um, Matt?"

He turned. His eyes met hers.

"I—I just wanted to say again how much tonight's party meant to me. Thank you."

He smiled. "I'm glad. Good night, Emily."

"Good night, Matt," she said softly.

When the bedroom door closed behind him, she came out of the bathroom and, resigned, placed the blue satin nightgown in her drawer and took out the cotton one.

It couldn't be more clear.

Matt had no desire to make love to her. She touched her stomach. Looked at herself in the mirror. *Really* looked at herself.

She sighed dejectedly. No wonder he wasn't interested. She'd been kidding herself thinking all it would take was a satin nightgown to make her look attractive.

Face it. Until you have the baby and get back some semblance of your figure, he isn't going to be interested.

But what if, even then, he showed no inclination to make love? Oh, but surely he would. After all, he was the one who had said he'd like to have more children, if she were willing. So he must be planning on a normal marriage one of these days.

Sighing again, she climbed into bed and turned off the light. She guessed she would just have to be patient and make the best of it and try not to act as if she minded that they weren't physically intimate.

But no matter how many times she told herself she could wait, that after the baby was born everything would be different, her mind continued to churn with doubts. She was still awake an hour later when she heard Matt quietly entering the bedroom. She kept her eyes shut and her breathing even so he'd think she was asleep. She couldn't help noticing how careful he was to keep from touching her when he got into bed.

The thought struck her that maybe he was sorry he'd married her, and it was all she could do to banish it.

Quit borrowing trouble.

That was another of her aunt Maybelle's favorite sayings.

Oh, Aunt Maybelle, how I wish you were here. You or Mom. Someone I could talk to about this. Someone who could give me some advice.

Maybe she should confide in Nell. But she knew

she wouldn't. Nell was a good friend—her best friend, in fact—but there were simply some things she couldn't tell Nell, and this was one of them. It was too personal. Too intimate. And too embarrassing. She'd just have to muddle through on her own and hope that eventually things would work out.

Matt fought to keep his resolve firm. August segued into September, and during the day he kept himself as busy as possible at work so he wouldn't have time to think about the situation with Emily. At night he encouraged her to go to bed early, using her pregnancy as an excuse. He would read or watch TV until he was sure she was asleep before joining her in their king-size bed. And he always made sure he was nowhere near when she was dressing or undressing.

Throughout September and into a blessedly cooler October, he continued to avoid any circumstance where he might be tempted to give in to the ever-present ache of desire and love warring within him.

Soon, he kept telling himself. Soon the baby will be born, and then things would be different. Right now sex was probably the last thing on Emily's mind, but afterward…afterward, he would woo her. He would do all kinds of romantic things, and he would show her how he felt about her.

What if doesn't matter? What if she never feels any different? What if, no matter what you do, she never loves you the way you want her to or wants you the way she wanted Stephen? What if she doesn't find you attractive? What if all she wants from you is friend-

ship and safety for her baby? Will you be able to stand it?

Once, Matt had thought he could. Once, he'd thought just being with her and taking care of her would be enough. Now he wasn't sure. He guessed he would just have to wait until the time came and see how he felt.

Because, in the end, what other choice did he have?

Every morning now, when Emily woke up, she'd wonder if today was the day. She'd seen Dr. Talbot a few days earlier and he'd said the baby had moved into position, so it could happen at any time.

She touched her burgeoning stomach. The baby moved, and Emily smiled. She was sure the baby was a girl. Why, she didn't know, because she'd told Dr. Talbot she didn't want to know the sex of the baby, even though he said he could tell from her ultrasound.

"How are you feeling this morning?" Matt said when she joined him in the kitchen. She was no longer going into the office with him. Starting last week, Pam had taken over Emily's job.

"My back aches, but other than that, I feel pretty good," Emily said. She poured herself a cup of decaf and took a sip. Just then, the baby shifted position, and she laughed. She laid her hand on top of her stomach. "Whew, this kid is really active right now." The baby was still moving around, and Emily's stomach moved accordingly.

Impulsively she walked over to where Matt stood. "Do you want to feel?" Taking his hand, she placed it on her stomach, and as she did, their eyes met. The baby rolled again. Something flared in the depths of his eyes, and Emily's heart began to thud. She couldn't look away. Time stilled while their gazes remained locked.

"Emily..." His voice sounded rough, and his gaze dropped to her mouth.

Suddenly she knew he was going to kiss her, and her heart went haywire. She trembled, leaning toward him, and her eyelids drifted down.

And at that very moment, just as his head began to lower, the phone rang.

They both jumped. The coffee Emily was still holding splashed over onto her cotton robe.

"Damn," Matt muttered as he stalked over to the phone. "It's gotta be someone calling in sick."

While Matt talked to Pete, his mechanic, who— Emily gleaned from the one-sided conversation—had the flu, she cleaned herself up, sponging her robe with cold water while fighting to get her emotions and disappointment under control.

Afterward, she wondered if Matt really would have kissed her if the phone hadn't interrupted them. Maybe she'd imagined the whole thing, because by the time he finished talking and hung up the phone, he acted as if nothing were at all different than it had been any other morning since their wedding. They ate their breakfast, he watched the weather channel to see what the day's forecast was, she packed him a lunch and he gave her a casual peck on the cheek before leaving for the office.

Emily spent the morning doing minor chores around the house, then fixed herself a light lunch of soup and a tuna sandwich. Afterward, she went into the living room. She sat with her feet propped up and pillows supporting her back and watched a rerun of an old TV show. After a moment or two, Lorelei hopped up beside her. Emily buried her hand into the cat's thick fur and scratched her head gently while the cat purred her contentment.

When the show was over, she gave into the urge to close her eyes and soon fell asleep. At three-thirty, she awakened to a sharp pain that started in her back and radiated around to her stomach.

"Oh," she said in surprise, scaring the cat, who hopped down, walking away with her head held high.

The pain went away after a few seconds, and Emily took a deep breath. She wondered if perhaps she were starting her labor. She looked at her watch, noting it was exactly 3:32. Then, carefully, she got out of the chair and headed for the bathroom.

Ten minutes later, she had another sharp pain. This time she timed its length. Seven seconds. Her breath came faster when it subsided, and again she took several deep breaths.

If I have another pain, I'm calling Dr. Talbot.

Emily walked slowly into the bedroom. Her back was really aching now. She checked her overnight bag, although it had been packed for days. When it was time to go to the hospital, the only things she needed to add were her toothbrush, shampoo, comb and makeup. Satisfied that everything was ready, she slowly walked across the hall to the nursery. Every time she looked at the room, her heart filled with happiness. It was so perfect. She knew it used to be Laurie's room, but that fact didn't seem to bother Matt, and Emily was glad, for the room was easily the brightest one in the house. It faced east, so it got the morning sun, but even in the afternoon it was lovely with a muted golden glow.

Months ago, Emily had settled on a circus motif and primary colors as the decorating scheme. Matt had painted the walls a sunny yellow, and on a trip into Fort Worth, Emily had found exactly the kind of border she'd envisioned, with circus animals in rich shades of candy apple red, kelly green, vibrant purple, royal blue and orange. Matching sheets and bumper pad adorned the crib, and a glittering circus mobile hung from the ceiling.

A white wicker rocking chair with bright red cushions, a white changing table with a royal blue coverlet, a white metal diaper pail and a white chest with a circus lamp completed the furnishings. Later, Emily planned to paint circus animals on a white toy box.

As she stood in the doorway admiring the room, another pain speared her. Her breath hitched, and she glanced at her watch. Exactly ten minutes since the last one. Waiting until the pain went away, she walked back into the master bedroom and picked up the portable phone.

She knew Dr. Talbot's number by heart. Patty put her right through.

Dr. Talbot listened as Emily described the pains.

"Head for the hospital," he said when she'd finished. "I'll call and tell them you're on your way. I'll be there when I'm finished up here."

"All right," Emily said, excitement causing her voice to tremble. As soon as the connection was severed, she called Matt.

"I'll be there in fifteen minutes," he said.

"Don't speed. There's plenty of time," she assured him.

He arrived in twelve minutes flat, breathless, blue eyes bright.

"You were speeding," she said in mock accusation.

"I couldn't help it." He lifted her bag, which she'd brought out to the kitchen. "This it?"

She nodded.

He put his arm around her shoulder and gave it a squeeze. "Scared?"

Looking up, she met his eyes. "A little," she admitted.

He smiled. "Me, too."

It took them twenty minutes to get to the county hospital, which was located just south of Fleming, the county seat. It was a small hospital with only sixty beds, ten of them in the maternity wing.

"Busy day today," the admitting nurse said. "You're the fourth expectant mom to arrive."

Two years earlier the hospital had remodeled and updated its maternity facilities and now had four individual birthing rooms instead of the old-fashioned delivery rooms. Emily was turned over to the maternity charge nurse, a cheerful-looking forty-something blonde with friendly gray eyes and a no-nonsense manner. "I'm Jenny," she said. "Let's get you settled in while we're waiting on your doctor."

For the next hour, Emily was hooked up to the monitor and poked and prodded and examined by several nurses and one harried intern.

"It's his first day here," Jenny confided. "He's in panic mode because we're so busy."

When Matt looked worried, she was quick to reassure him. "Don't worry. He's a good doctor. He'll settle down when he realizes he knows what he's doing."

By now Emily's pains were coming every seven minutes and she'd been assigned a nurse, this one a tall brunette with kind blue eyes behind black-rimmed granny glasses named Kasey. "You're progressing nicely," she declared, fussing around Emily's bed.

Matt was fascinated with the monitor, which allowed them to hear the baby's heartbeat and see the pulse rate. He sat close to Emily's bedside and held her hand, coaching her through each pain, all the while watching and listening to the monitor.

"This is your first baby, isn't it?" Kasey said.

"Yes," Emily said.

Matt averted his gaze, and Emily wondered what he was feeling right then.

"First babies are always so much fun," Kasey added, smiling. "Are you having a boy or a girl?"

"We don't know," Emily said, gasping as another pain hit.

Kasey timed the pain. "We're down to five minutes apart."

Emily bit her lip. This pain was harder and sharper than any that had come before. Matt squeezed her hand.

Just then Dr. Talbot walked into the room. He washed his hands and pulled on thin rubber gloves. When he was finished examining Emily, he nodded in satisfaction. "Things are looking good. Shouldn't be long now."

The next thirty minutes would ever after be a blur in Emily's mind. The pains came faster and stronger and soon she was urged to push. Matt steadfastly stood at her side, encouraging her and giving her strength when she felt she couldn't do it any longer.

"C'mon, Emily," Dr. Talbot said. "You can do it. With the next contraction, bear down and push as hard as you can."

Emily squeezed her eyes shut and concentrated. And when the next contraction hit, she gave it everything she had, gritting her teeth and groaning as she pushed and pushed some more. She held on to Matt's hand as hard as she could, taking comfort from his solidity and strength.

"The baby's out!" the doctor said triumphantly.

Emily sank back against her pillow, exhausted. "Wh-what is it?"

Matt leaned over and kissed her cheek. "It's a girl," he said. "A beautiful girl."

Suddenly all Emily's exhaustion vanished, and she

was filled with the deepest joy and thankfulness. "Let me see."

"In a minute. Let's get her cleaned up," Kasey said.

Later, as Emily gazed into her daughter's brilliant eyes—Stephen's eyes—and touched the soft tufts of black hair on her head—Stephen's hair—she was filled with a wonder bordering on awe.

"She's wonderful, isn't she?" she said to Matt.

His smile was tender and loving. "Yes, she is. Just like her mother."

"Oh, Matt. What a sweet thing to say."

"It's true."

"Matt..." Emily hesitated, wondering how he was going to take what she planned to say.

"What?"

"Would...would you mind terribly if we named the baby Stephanie?"

He shook his head quickly. Almost too quickly, Emily thought. The last thing she wanted to do was hurt Matt. And yet...this child was so like her father, and it just seemed fitting she should be named for him.

"I don't mind at all," Matt said.

She searched his eyes, but all she saw was sincerity. Her heart lifted in relief. "Thanks, Matt," she said softly.

A few minutes later Kasey came in to take Stephanie to the nursery where she would be bathed and tagged and weighed and dressed in a clean gown. "I'll be back in a little while to get you cleaned up, too," she told Emily, "so you'll look nice and pretty for your visitors."

"That's right," Matt said. "I'd better go call Pam and Nell right now, or they'll skin me alive." He turned to follow Kasey and the baby from the room, then stopped. "Anyone else you want me to call?"

Their eyes met, and she knew he was thinking of Cornelia. She shook her head. "She'll hear soon enough."

"Miz Pierce? Telephone for you."

Cornelia frowned. It was after eleven. Who on earth was calling her this late at night? She accepted the portable phone from Rosella and waited until the housekeeper left the room before saying hello.

"Cornelia?" It was Lucas Talbot.

"Lucas?"

"Thought you'd like to know that Emily had a baby girl earlier this evening."

Cornelia's heart beat faster. "I see. Is...is everything all right?"

"Both mother and baby are doing fine."

"Where are they? At County General?"

"Yes. If all goes well, they'll be released tomorrow afternoon, though."

"So if I want to see the baby, I'd better get over there in the morning."

"Yes."

"Well, thank you, Lucas. And did you take care of that matter I asked you to?"

There was a long silence.

"Lucas?" she said sharply. "Did you?"

"Not yet, Cornelia. Why don't you go over and see the baby first? Then, if you still want me to, we'll talk."

"There's nothing to talk about. We've already settled it."

"Just go on over in the morning, okay?"

"It won't change anything." When he didn't reply, she sighed. "Oh, all right, Lucas. All right. I'll humor you this once. But I'm not going to change my mind."

After they hung up she sat silently, thinking. *Oh, Stephen, if only you were here. If this baby is really yours, this should be the happiest day of our lives. We should be celebrating right now.*

Cornelia never cried. She considered tears a sign of weakness, and she was not a weak woman. She hadn't even cried when she'd been told about Stephen's death. Yet right then she felt closer to tears than she had since she was a child.

She struggled not to give in to them. What good would tears do? They would change nothing.

Stephen was dead.

But maybe, just maybe, a part of him still lived.

Chapter Eleven

Cornelia arrived at the hospital at eight o'clock the following morning. She found the maternity wing and the nursery with no problem.

Her heart beat faster as she peered through the glass window. There were two babies in the nursery. One was being bathed by a nurse. Since the child was quite obviously a boy, Cornelia turned her attention to the other baby, which was lying in its little bed. Attached to the bed was a card that clearly said Thompson.

She took one good look and knew DNA testing would not be necessary. Swallowing against the unaccustomed lump in her throat, she studied the infant. No one could deny the child was Stephen's. Why, the baby looked exactly like him, from the tufts of black hair on her head, to her bright eyes which were already turning green, to the deep dimples in her cheeks.

Cornelia struggled to contain her emotions as she drank in every inch of her new granddaughter. Images flashed through her mind, one after another. Stephen, on the day she'd given birth to him. Her disappointment the day her doctor had told her she wouldn't ever bear another child. The plans she'd made for Stephen. How she'd envisioned three or four healthy, happy grandchildren on the ranch, children that would carry on the proud Pierce tradition.

Standing there, a fierce love consumed her, and she knew she would do anything, *anything,* to have this child, to raise her as a Pierce should be raised.

Just then, a freckle-faced, redheaded nurse entered the nursery. Smiling at Cornelia, she walked over to Stephen's baby and lifted her from her bed. Then she walked to the door.

"I'll bet you're this little one's grandmother," she said when she came out.

"Yes," said Cornelia, "I am." She walked closer. She felt absurdly close to tears again as she stared down in wonder mixed with sadness at the realization that Stephen would never see his child.

"You can touch her," the nurse said kindly.

Cornelia's finger trembled as she reached out and gently stroked the baby's cheek. The skin was unbelievably soft. Something squeezed Cornelia's heart, and she swallowed hard.

"I'm just about to take her to her mother's room."

The nurse smiled encouragingly as she started down the hall.

Cornelia followed. She hadn't intended to see Emily today, but she couldn't bring herself to leave. Who knew how long it would be before she could see the baby again?

About halfway down the hall, the nurse stopped and knocked softly on the door to room 23, then opened the door and went in.

"Here's your little daughter come to visit," the nurse said.

Cornelia heard Emily reply, then a deeper rumble she recognized as Matt's voice. Jaw hardening, she walked into the room, and just as she did, the nurse handed the baby to Matt.

"Why don't we let your daddy hold you for a minute until I get your mama set up to nurse?" the nurse said.

The word *daddy* was like a match set to dry kindling. Something inside Cornelia erupted, and she charged across the room and tried to take the baby away from the nurse, but the shocked nurse held on tight. Cornelia's voice shook with fury. "He is *not* her father! My dead son is her father. I will *not* allow him to be referred to as this child's father, not by you, not by anyone!"

The nurse's mouth dropped open.

Cornelia ignored her, turning her gaze to Emily. Emily, white-faced, looked from Cornelia to Matt.

After seconds of stunned silence, Matt said, "I want you to leave."

Cornelia jerked around, ready to tell him just what she thought of him and his orders, but something in his eyes stopped her. She contented herself with saying, "This isn't the end, you know." Turning back to Emily, she said, "You'd better take very good care of my granddaughter or you'll answer to me."

Emily hesitated, then said softly, "Her name is Stephanie."

It took every bit of strength and will that Cornelia possessed not to flinch or betray by even the flicker of her eyes that what Emily had said had affected her deeply.

After one last glance in the baby's direction, Cornelia spun on her heel and, head held high, she left.

Emily sagged back against her pillow. She felt utterly drained by the scene with Cornelia.

"Oh, my goodness," said the nurse, her brown eyes wide.

"It's a damned good thing she left," Matt said through gritted teeth. "Else I wouldn't have been responsible for my actions." He reached for the baby. "Here, I'll take her now."

The nurse handed the baby over, then turned to Emily.

"I'm sorry you had to be a witness to that..." Emily glanced at the nurse's name tag. "Cindy, is it?"

Cindy nodded. "Gee, she sure was mad." Her eyes were filled with curiosity.

"She's hurting, that's the reason."

"My wife is too generous," Matt said. "Cornelia

Pierce is a vindictive, hateful, old...*woman* who is used to having her own way.''

"Matt," Emily said. She knew he'd been about to say *bitch* but had caught himself in time.

"It's the truth, Emily. I don't care if she *is* hurting. That's no reason to act the way she does."

By now Cindy had gotten Emily ready for the baby, and she took her from Matt and placed her in Emily's arms. Immediately the tension caused by Cornelia faded away, and Emily was filled with a warm contentment. She smiled down at the baby.

"Okay, let's get you started. Have you tried nursing yet?" Cindy said.

"Once during the night, but it didn't seem to work very well."

"It's hard, the first time you try," Cindy said. "But it's worth doing, you know. Even if you can only nurse for a week or two, it gives your baby a wonderful start in life."

"Oh, I know," Emily said. "I want to nurse. It's just that I don't think she was getting much. She got all frustrated and started crying."

"Well, let's try again." She helped Emily get her nipple into the baby's mouth, then turned to Matt, who was sitting back against the windowsill watching. "Mr. Thompson, it's real, real important not to upset Mrs. Thompson while she's nursing the baby, so I think you should try to keep the grandmother away until she calms down."

"Consider it done," Matt said.

* * *

Cornelia drove home too fast. So fast, in fact, she nearly had an accident on the outskirts of San Pedro. The near miss scared her, and she finally slowed down. But she didn't calm down. She couldn't.

Daddy.

She still felt outraged at the thought that that stupid nurse had referred to Matt Thompson as Stephanie's father. And if the baby were raised by him, that's the way *everyone* would eventually think of him, even if they knew better.

"Never," she muttered as she parked the pickup around the back of the house. "Never. Stephen's baby will *not* be raised by Matt Thompson. She is a *Pierce.*"

She ignored Rosella's curious expression as she walked through the back door and into the big kitchen and headed straight for her study. Picking up the phone, she called Walker Nesbitt.

"Good morning, Cornelia," he said when his secretary put him on the line.

"Walker, I want you to find me the best private investigator you can. Money is no object."

After a few moments of silence, Walker said, "Care to tell me what's goin' on?"

"Emily had her baby last night. I went to see it this morning. The child is definitely Stephen's."

"And?"

"And I want to proceed with what we discussed. Emily will be taking the baby home today. I want her watched. I want evidence I can use to show she's unfit to raise my granddaughter."

"Cornelia...don't you think—"

"No, Walker, I don't *think* anything. I know. Just do as I say."

"All right, Cornelia," he said in a resigned voice. "I'll find you an investigator."

The investigator's name was Travis O'Malley. He was a short, nondescript man with graying hair and pale blue eyes behind thick bifocals. At first Cornelia was put off by his appearance. How could such a colorless person be smart enough for the job she wanted done? But ten minutes in his presence changed her mind. It was obvious to her that O'Malley purposely opted for his fade-into-the-background persona. And equally obvious that his amorphous facade disguised a keen intellect and sharp mind.

"I'll give you weekly reports," he said as they wrapped up their meeting.

"Good."

"And don't worry, Mrs. Pierce," he added. "If there's anything at all to be found, I'll find it."

Emily adored her little daughter. And she loved having her at home, in the bright nursery prepared so lovingly. But it wasn't easy adjusting, for either one of them.

Unfortunately, Emily was still having problems nursing Stephanie, and she'd finally had to resort to a breast pump, but even that didn't work for long, because she simply didn't have much milk.

"Sometimes it happens that way," Dr. Talbot said. "Some mothers just can't nurse."

"Is there nothing we can do?"

"I'm afraid not, Emily. Let's try her on formula. She'll be happier, and it'll certainly be easier on you."

The first formula they tried disagreed with Stephanie, and they had to switch. Just when Emily thought they'd finally found something that worked, the baby developed colic.

Day after day, all Stephanie did was cry. She'd scrunch up her little face until it was all red and she'd shriek.

By mid-November when Stephanie was three weeks old, Emily was beside herself. Where most new mothers were able to get at least three or four hours sleep at a stretch, Emily was only able to catnap, because Stephanie never slept more than an hour at a time. And when she was awake, the only way Emily could keep her calm and quiet was by walking her.

Before long, Emily was exhausted. She had deep circles under her eyes, and she was losing weight.

Too much weight, Matt thought. He was worried about Emily. If only she had someone to help her—a sister or a mother. He suggested hiring a nurse to come in, at least during the day, but Emily wouldn't hear of it.

"No," she said. "Stephanie is my responsibility, Matt."

Matt knew that in some skewed way, Emily felt

she would not be a good mother if she abdicated responsibility for the baby. But something had to be done. Emily couldn't go on this way.

There was one bright spot in the three weeks since they'd brought the baby home, though. At least Cornelia Pierce had not tried to contact them again.

"Maybe she's given up," Emily said hopefully.

Fat chance, Matt thought, but he didn't say so. Emily had enough to worry about. If she had convinced herself they had no more to fear from Cornelia, he was glad.

A couple of nights before Thanksgiving, they had a particularly bad night. Stephanie cried from ten o'clock on. At three in the morning, Matt got up and walked into the nursery. Emily was sitting in the rocking chair, the baby in her arms. They were both asleep, but Emily's head had fallen forward, and Matt knew she must be terribly uncomfortable. His heart contracted as he looked at her. He loved her so much. Softly, so as not to awaken the baby, he touched Emily's shoulder.

"Wha—?" She was instantly awake, her eyes filled with fear.

"Let me take Stephanie," he said. "You go to bed."

She started to protest, but he wouldn't listen. He reached for the baby. "Now go."

Stephanie stirred and whimpered when he took her, so he walked her around the room until she'd settled down again. An hour later, feeling the baby's sleep was sound enough, he gently laid her in the crib. He held his breath, but she didn't awaken.

He watched her sleep for a few minutes, thinking how completely vulnerable babies were and how much he loved her. He knew now that the emptiness he sometimes still felt over the loss of Laurie would never go away completely. But Stephanie's coming had made a difference.

A few minutes later, he quietly rejoined Emily in their bed. She was sleeping on her side, facing him, and as the bed shifted under his weight, she sighed and snuggled close to him.

Matt froze. It was sheer torment to feel her there. Her warmth, her feminine scent, the curves of her body that fit so perfectly against him. He'd loved her for so long. Wanted her for so long.

It was all he could do to keep from putting his arms around her. But he knew he must not. Emily hadn't had her six-week checkup yet, so even if she were emotionally ready for sexual intimacy, she wasn't physically.

Resolutely, Matt turned away. But it was a long time before he fell asleep again.

The following morning, when Emily awakened, she stretched luxuriously. She felt better than she'd felt in weeks. It had been so wonderful to have some uninterrupted sleep. She stretched again. It was so blessedly quiet. Stephanie must still be sleeping. Sighing, Emily turned over and looked at the bedside clock. It read 9:46.

Good heavens, 9:46! It was so late! Matt should have left for work hours ago. She jumped up and reached for her robe, hurrying across to the nursery to check on the baby. The nursery was empty. Her heart jumped in alarm. Where was Matt? Where was Stephanie?

She rushed down the hall and into the kitchen, then stopped dead. She rubbed her eyes, sure she was imagining the scene before her. Matt was sitting at the kitchen table, sipping at a mugful of coffee and talking to Stephanie, who—unbelievably—was quietly sitting in her infant carrier, which Matt had placed near his chair. And she was kicking and smiling and cooing at him!

Emily couldn't believe it. Amazed and delighted, she walked slowly forward. Matt raised his eyes and smiled. "Good morning."

"Hi. What's going on here?"

He looked at Stephanie, touching her hand with his forefinger. Her tiny fingers immediately curled around his. "Well," he drawled, "this little lady and I are having a nice, long talk."

Emily grinned. "Oh, really? About what?"

"Oh, this and that." His eyes looked bluer than usual this morning as they once more met hers. "Mainly that."

Emily laughed. "I can't believe how happy she is. And how quiet."

"I know."

"What did you do? Give her some magic potion?"

He shook his head. "Nope. She just woke up

happy. When I woke up, I heard her gurgling in her crib, so I went in and changed her diaper and brought her out here and fixed her a bottle. She drank it all, too. And ever since, we've been getting to know each other." He looked enormously proud of himself.

"I can't believe it." This was the first morning Stephanie hadn't awakened crying. "But, Matt, I feel bad about it being so late. You should have been at the office hours ago."

"No problem. I called Pam and told her I probably wouldn't be in before noon. She doesn't care. We probably won't be busy today. Not with Thanksgiving tomorrow."

Just then, Stephanie made another cooing sound and kicked her feet.

"I just can't get over how contented she is. How long have the two of you been awake?"

"Since eight."

Almost two hours ago. And the baby hadn't cried in all that time. "This is wonderful. I'm almost afraid to speak to her, she seems so content." But she couldn't resist, because the baby looked so adorable sitting there. Emily leaned over and kissed Stephanie's head, inhaling the sweet baby smell. "Hi, sweetheart."

Stephanie looked up at her, then turned her attention back to Matt. Emily might have been jealous except that she was so thrilled to see a calm, happy baby instead of one who couldn't seem to stop crying. "She likes you," she said softly.

Matt smiled. "I like her, too." He inclined his head. "There's fresh coffee on the counter."

"Do you mind if I go and brush my teeth and hair first? I was kind of alarmed when I woke up and Stephanie wasn't in her crib, so I came right out."

"Why would I mind?"

"Okay. I'll just be a couple of minutes."

"Take your time. We're not going anywhere, are we, Short Stuff?"

Smiling, Emily headed for the bedroom. She decided she might as well get dressed while she was at it, so once she finished in the bathroom, she put on jeans and a long-sleeved yellow cotton blouse and tied her hair back with a yellow ribbon. She even put on some lipstick, and she was amazed at how much better she looked.

"I like the ribbon," Matt said when she rejoined him in the kitchen. There was an admiring gleam in his eyes.

"Thank you, sir." Emily walked to the counter and poured herself coffee. His expression gave her a tingly feeling, and she thought how in just a little over a week she was due for her six-week checkup. And then... The direction of her thoughts flustered her. To cover her agitation, she hurriedly said, "Are you hungry? Have you had any breakfast?"

"Yes, I'm hungry, and no, I haven't had breakfast. Too busy with Short Stuff here."

"How about if I make some waffles before you go in to work?"

"Sounds great." Matt stretched, and when he did,

his dark blue T-shirt tightened over his chest and arm muscles.

A funny, achy feeling stole through Emily, and her breath came faster. Flustered, she walked over to the pantry for the waffle mix, then to the refrigerator for the eggs and milk. All the while, she was acutely aware of him behind her. She knew he was watching her, and she felt self-conscious.

She had just broken eggs into a bowl and was measuring the mix when the telephone rang. She glanced at Matt to see if he wanted her to get it, but he had already gotten up. "It's probably Pam." He gestured toward the baby, who had fallen asleep.

She looked like an angel, Emily thought, smiling. So sweet and innocent. She thought about moving her, then decided to leave well enough alone. She was perfectly safe in her infant carrier, and it was so wonderful to have her quiet and contented.

Matt lifted the receiver. "Hello." After a second or two, his voice changed. "Jeff! It's about time you called. Where the hell have you been?"

Emily listened to the one-sided conversation as she continued with her waffle preparation. She knew Matt must be enormously relieved to have finally heard from his brother.

"What?" Matt was saying. "You've been *where?*"

Emily turned around. Matt looked shocked. Something must be seriously wrong. Fear for him caused her throat to go dry.

"God, Jeff, I can't believe you would do something

so stupid!'' Matt's eyes met hers, and he shook his head in disbelief.

Relieved because Matt seemed disgusted rather than fearful, Emily went back to making her waffles, all the while wondering what Jeff was telling Matt.

Matt listened for a long time, only interjecting an occasional, ''I see.'' Finally he said, ''Well, little brother, I hope you learned something from all of this.'' He listened a few more seconds, then said, ''Look, I'd like to say yes, but, well, some things have changed here since I last heard from you. The thing is, I've gotten married. Yeah, you heard right. No, you've never met her, but I told you about her when she first started working for me. Yeah, it's Emily. Yeah. So I can't give you an answer right now. I'll have to talk to her about this first, because it affects her, too. Give me a number where I can reach you, and after she and I talk, I'll call you back. Okay? Okay.'' Matt reached for the notepad they kept by the phone and scrawled something on it, then said goodbye.

Emily finished pouring batter into the waffle iron before turning to look at Matt.

He looked at her gravely.

''What is it, Matt?''

He shook his head again. ''You know, sometimes you just wonder how three people born to the same parents could be so different.''

Emily waited.

Matt sighed. ''The reason we haven't heard from Jeff is he's been in prison.''

"Prison!"

"Well, actually it was a county work facility, minimum security."

"But why? What did he do?"

"He got busted for growing marijuana. Seems he had his whole backyard planted with the stuff and was making a tidy little living selling it." He was shaking his head again. "God, I just can't believe he was so *stupid!*"

The waffle iron sizzled, and Emily removed the cooked waffle and poured in fresh batter. She closed the lid, then turned her attention back to Matt.

"He was sentenced to a year, but because of good behavior, they let him go after six months. He's on parole now."

Now it was Emily's turn to shake her head. She knew how Matt must feel. Even though he'd seen little of his brother in the recent past, he cared about him.

"He wants to come here," Matt said.

Emily smiled. "Well, that's good, isn't it?"

"You may not think so when I tell you everything."

"Tell me."

"As a condition of parole, he has to have a place to live and a job. He wants to work for me and live with us."

"Is that a problem?"

Matt studied her for a minute. "Does that mean you don't mind?"

"Oh, Matt, of course, I don't mind," Emily said

with no hesitation. After all Matt had done for her, this was a very small thing he was asking. "Jeff is your brother. Of course, we must help him. Everyone deserves a second chance."

Matt studied her for a long moment. Then he smiled. "Have I told you lately what a wonderful person you are?"

Emily could feel herself blushing, and she busied herself removing the second cooked waffle. "I'm not wonderful."

"Well, we won't argue the point, but I just want you to know how much I appreciate this."

Emily looked up again. "Matt, family is family. Now, why don't you call him back and tell him we want him?"

For the rest of the day, each time Emily thought about Matt's reaction to her agreement that Jeff should come to San Pedro and live with them, she was filled with a warm, happy glow.

Somehow, today, they had turned a corner. With Stephanie. With their marriage. With their very lives. She even felt optimistic that the bad times with Cornelia were behind them, since they'd heard nothing from her after that terrible scene in the hospital.

Emily's normal cautiousness was swept away, and even though she knew she was tempting fate, she couldn't help feeling that from now on life was only going to get better.

Chapter Twelve

Emily, Matt and Stephanie spent Thanksgiving with Pam and Ben and the boys. Emily had been dreading the holiday because she and Stephen were married right before Thanksgiving last year, but going to Pam's where it was noisy and filled with happy sounds helped dispel any sadness that might be lurking, just waiting to attack Emily when she least expected it.

It also helped that Thanksgiving was another good day for Stephanie. Since the episode with Matt the previous morning, her crying spells hadn't come as often or lasted as long. Emily mentally crossed her fingers that maybe Stephanie's colic was over. Or at least not as severe as it had been the past few weeks.

When they arrived, Stephanie was asleep.

"My kids always fell asleep in the car, too," Pam said. "I put up the playpen in our bedroom. You can lay her down in there."

That was Pam. Prepared for every contingency, Emily thought with affection and amusement. "Thanks, Pam. I'll just put the whole carrier in the playpen." Emily had the kind of infant car seat where all you had to do was release the locks and the seat part came out, making a convenient carrier.

They got the baby settled without waking her and headed back to the dining room.

Pam loved to entertain, and Emily saw she had gone all out for Thanksgiving.

"It's my favorite holiday," she said happily.

The table looked beautiful, with a centerpiece of fall flowers that had come from Pam's garden, flanked by ornate silver candlesticks—"They were Mom's," Pam told Emily—and all the usual Thanksgiving fare: turkey, dressing, cranberry sauce, mashed potatoes, sweet potatoes, peas, hot rolls and gravy. Emily's contributions were a fresh fruit salad, a marinated vegetable salad and an apple pie. Pam had also made pumpkin and pecan pies.

"Honey," Ben said, laughing and holding his stomach when the meal was over, "are you women trying to kill us with all this food?"

"Hey, we didn't tell you to have a second helping of everything," Pam countered, giving Emily one of her these-men-what-can-you-do-with-them looks.

Emily smothered a smile.

"I wanted to have plenty of leftovers," Pam explained. "'Cause I plan to send some of everything home with Matt and Emily. After all, Jeff arrives tomorrow, and you know how he's always liked to eat."

Jeff's imminent arrival had injected an extra dose of festivity into the day. Emily could see that Pam was already anticipating someone else to mother.

Later, as they were getting ready to leave for home, Pam pulled Emily aside. "Emily, if you have any reservations at all about Jeff staying with you, it's not too late to change your mind. Ben and I discussed it, and we'd be happy to have him here."

"That's sweet of you, Pam, but I don't mind at all. Actually, I'm kind of looking forward to getting to know Jeff."

That part was true, but Emily did have some reservations. After all, Jeff was an unknown quantity. Maybe she wouldn't like him. Or maybe he wouldn't like her. There could be any number of problems. But she would never admit any of this to Pam, because she didn't want Matt to know. She felt strongly that after everything he had done for her, welcoming his brother into their home was a very small thing to do in return.

"Well, if you change your mind..." Pam said. "The offer's open."

Emily smiled and gave Pam a hug. "Thanks. I really appreciate it."

That night, once Stephanie was fed and bathed and—Emily fervently hoped—asleep for at least a few hours, she joined Matt in the living room and told him about Pam's offer. "It was nice of her, wasn't it?"

Matt gave her a cynical look. "Well, yeah, but her motives aren't entirely unselfish, you know."

"Why do you say that?"

"Because I know Pam. She'd like nothing better than to get her hooks into Jeff."

"Don't you think it's natural that she'd want to mother him? After all, she *is* fourteen years older."

"Smother him is more like it. Order him around like she does her kids."

"Now, Matt," Emily chided mildly. "That's not fair. Pam might be a little bossy, but she only has the best interests of her family at heart. You know that."

"I'm sure that's true, but the problem is she thinks she knows best—about everything—and she doesn't. She'd drive Jeff crazy in a week, maybe sooner. It's bad enough he screwed up and we all know it. He doesn't need her reminding him constantly. Plus, he's going to be working around her all day. That's enough of Pam for anyone." Suddenly he frowned. "You aren't having second thoughts, are you?"

"No! That's not why I told you about Pam. I meant what I said yesterday. Jeff can stay with us as long as he wants to."

"Okay, good," he said in obvious relief. "And I promise you, Emily, it won't be long. Knowing Jeff, he'll want to get an apartment of his own as soon as he can. And, hey, that's understandable. A young, single guy—we're bound to cramp his style...even in a town as unexciting as San Pedro."

"I thought one of the conditions of the parole board allowing him to leave California was that he had to live with family."

"No, he just had to have a place to live and a job to go to." When Emily didn't answer right away, he picked up the morning paper and began to browse through it. Within minutes, something caught his eye, and he began to read.

Emily thought about everything he'd said. One thing niggled at her, and finally she said, "Matt..."

"Hmm?" He looked up.

"Does it bother *you* to have Pam in the office all day?"

He lowered the paper. "No, not really. She's a good worker, and she caught on to the office routine fast. As far as the other stuff goes...shoot, I just ignore her."

"But you said Jeff—"

"I know, but it's different with Jeff. He never could ignore anyone. He used to get all bent out of shape when we tried to tell him anything and go stomping off. Of course, he was a lot younger then, and kids tend to be that way. Hopefully he's matured some and will have more tolerance." He smiled. "Now don't *you* start worrying about me, Emily. As I'm always telling Pam, I'm a grown man. I can take care of myself."

"I know that, Matt. I guess I just can't help feeling a little bit guilty about deserting you in the office."

"Now listen to me. You haven't deserted me. You

are exactly where I want you to be. Here…in our home…as my wife.''

His words warmed her, because she could see he meant them. But they also reminded her that she wasn't *really* his wife, not the way she wanted to be, and now, with his brother coming, she was afraid intimacy would continue to elude them.

I won't let it, she told herself determinedly. *As soon as the doctor says we can, I will do everything in my power to be a real wife to Matt, Jeff or no Jeff.*

Despite Emily's assurances about Jeff and her willingness to have him there, Matt couldn't help worrying. Another adult in the house was bound to cause problems for them. Lack of privacy alone would take some getting used to.

But, as he'd told Emily, he didn't expect the situation to last long. In fact, Matt hoped that by the time Emily had her six-week checkup, Jeff would have found a place and be gone.

Her six-week checkup.

Matt couldn't wait.

Somehow he had survived the past eight months. Somehow he had found the strength to keep his hands off her without going crazy from need and desire. And somehow he would get through the next couple of weeks…or however long it took for her to be ready to make their marriage a true one in every sense of the word.

Maybe having Jeff there would actually make these

last few weeks of waiting easier. Matt hoped so. He didn't see how they could possibly be any harder.

The following day Matt left at noon to get Jeff, and it was four o'clock before he got back. Emily was sitting in the living room feeding Stephanie a bottle when she heard the crunch of gravel in the driveway that signaled the Bronco's return. Getting up, she walked with the baby to the window overlooking the backyard and watched Matt and a slightly smaller, younger version of her husband unloading bags from the back of the truck.

It was a sunny, cool day—a lot like California weather, Emily imagined—and Jeff was dressed for it in jeans, boots and a white cable-knit sweater. Matt, too, wore jeans, boots and a sweater, only his was dark green. Emily admired the way they both looked.

When they turned around, Matt spied her standing at the window. He grinned, and she smiled back.

A few seconds later, the two men came inside. Seeing Jeff up close gave her a jolt, he looked so much like his older brother. Same deep blue eyes, same sun-weathered face, same square jaw, same light brown hair streaked with gold. But when he smiled, she saw the difference. Jeff's smile was bold, almost cocky, whereas Matt's came slower and with quieter confidence.

"Emily, this is Jeff," Matt was saying. "Jeff, my wife, Emily, and our new little daughter, Stephanie." His voice rang with quiet pride.

Since Jeff didn't raise any eyebrows, Emily figured

Matt had explained the situation with the baby before reaching the house.

"Hi, Jeff," she said. "Welcome home." She propped the baby's bottle under her chin to free her right hand.

He put down his bags and took it, grinning at her all the while. "Just as pretty as I thought she'd be." He gave Matt a sidelong look. "Too pretty for you."

A natural charmer, too, Emily thought in amusement.

Matt chuckled. "Just don't get any ideas."

"Hey, can't blame a man for looking."

"Sure you can," Matt said.

Emily could feel her face heating. "You're embarrassing me."

Now they both laughed.

"And lookit here," Jeff said. His smile became softer as his gaze moved to the baby. He touched Stephanie's cheek. "Hey, there, Stephanie. It's your uncle Jeff. Aren't you a cutie pie?" He leaned over and kissed her forehead. As he straightened, his eyes met Emily's again. "She's great," he said. "Can I hold her?"

In that instant, Jeff won Emily's heart. "Sure. But don't you want to put your things in your room first?"

Later, watching him with the baby, Emily thought about how, although she was uncertain about many things in life, she was sure about one: Matt's brother didn't have a bad bone in his body. He had gotten into trouble because he acted impulsively, making decisions without thinking of consequences.

It was going to be okay having him there. Maybe even more than okay.

Cornelia had just about reached the point of letting Travis O'Malley go. In the past month, he had found nothing. Not one single thing.

"I don't know what I'm paying you for," she said when she'd read his latest report. "There's nothing here that's useful." She threw it down in disgust.

"Well, ma'am, I can't manufacture something that doesn't exist," he replied mildly, obviously not the least bit perturbed by her criticism.

Cornelia gave him a hard-eyed stare, the one that intimidated most people. "Well, I *can't* believe Emily is so squeaky-clean. Everyone has *something* to hide. You're just not digging deep enough."

O'Malley returned her glare with a thoughtful look. "Ordinarily I would agree with you, Mrs. Pierce, because in my line of work, if I've learned anything, I've learned that most people have a dark side. However, in this case, I'm beginning to believe your former daughter-in-law is exactly what she appears to be: a decent young woman who has worked hard all of her life and always tried to do the right thing."

Cornelia pressed her lips together to keep herself from making the stinging retort she wanted to make. Whose side was O'Malley on, anyway? she thought furiously. She was beginning to wonder if he was really as good as he was touted to be. Sure couldn't prove it by what he'd done so far.

"I personally think continued surveillance of the

Thompsons is a waste of my time and your money,"
O'Malley continued, "but if you want me to keep it
up, I will."

As satisfying as it would have been to give him his
walking papers, Cornelia knew she couldn't. That
would mean she was giving up. And giving up meant
she could only see Stephanie once a month or however often the courts decreed, and that was completely
unacceptable. "Until I tell you otherwise, I want to
know everything that goes on in that house. Everything."

He shrugged. "You're the boss."

The moment he was gone, she called Walker Nesbitt. "Are you sure that so-called investigator you
sent me knows what he's doing?"

"Jack Sherman says O'Malley is the best investigator available."

Cornelia knew that Sherman was an assistant dis-
trict attorney in Fort Worth who had supposedly used
O'Malley many times. "Well, he can't be that good!
He hasn't found one blasted thing of value."

"Cornelia, these things take time," Walker replied.
"You've got to learn to be more patient. I assure you,
if there's anything to find, O'Malley will find it."

"He'd better, because I'm only going to give him
another week or so, and if he hasn't dug up anything
by then, you'll have to find me someone who will."

Four days later O'Malley called. "Someone new
has moved into the Thompsons' house."

Cornelia had been entering figures into her household ledger, but now her hand stilled and she put down her pen. "Oh? Who?"

"From what I can gather, it's Matt Thompson's younger brother."

"Jeff?" Cornelia remembered Jeff. He'd been a little older than Stephen and a real hell-raiser as a kid. As far as she knew, he'd been in California for years. "So what? He's probably just come to visit."

"No, I don't think so. He's been working for Thompson at the airfield. I talked to one of the flying instructors, and he said it was his understanding that the brother was back in San Pedro to stay."

That was certainly interesting. Cornelia wondered what had brought Jeff back. San Pedro was a far cry from the kinds of places he was probably used to. In fact, she couldn't imagine why he'd want to return.

"This could be the break we've been waiting for," O'Malley went on.

"How so?"

"Well, the talk is he was in some kind of trouble out on the coast."

"What kind?"

"I don't know. And there's no way to find out here. What I'd like is your permission to go out to L.A. and investigate."

It didn't take more than a second or two for Cornelia to see the possible value of his suggestion. "Fine. Go. But you'd better come back with something good."

"Look, Mrs. Pierce, let's get something straight, okay? Just because you order me to do something doesn't mean it's going to happen. Sure, I'll dig around and find out anything there is to find out. But whether it'll be something 'good' as you call it, is not something I can control.''

Cornelia's jaw clenched.

''Mrs. Pierce?''

''I heard you.''

''And we understand each other?''

''We understand each other,'' she finally said, but grudgingly.

''Good. I'll call you as soon as I get there.''

Jeff settled into the household easily, almost as if he'd always lived there. He was no trouble. He was neat and, after the first day or so, when he knew where things were and how she ran the house, he pitched in without being asked.

Emily enjoyed having him around. She admitted to herself that one of the reasons she liked him so much was that he reminded her of Stephen. He had the same charm and recklessness. And he made her laugh.

He was also wonderful with Stephanie. It was obvious to Emily that he had fallen in love with the baby. And Stephanie reciprocated. Even when she was at her fussiest, if Jeff took her and talked to her, she would usually calm down.

''You're so good with her,'' Emily said.

''I've always liked kids.''

''It shows.''

One night he suggested that Matt take Emily out

to dinner while he baby-sat Stephanie. At first, Emily resisted.

"C'mon, Emily," he urged, "you can trust me."

"It's not that. It's just…" Emily's voice trailed off. She looked at Matt helplessly.

"It's just that Emily thinks she'll be a bad mother if she thinks about herself, even for one minute," Matt teased.

"Oh, all right," Emily said.

So Matt took her to Sylvia's and plied her with two margaritas, which gave Emily a nice buzz and allowed her to relax in a way she hadn't for a long time.

"This is nice," she said. She finished the last bite of her sopaipilla and sat back in the booth, sated and happy. "I'm glad you talked me into this."

Matt smiled at her. "I am, too."

As they were driving home, Emily wished she'd already had her six-week checkup. But even if she had, how could they make love with Jeff in the house? She flinched thinking how close their bedroom was to his and how easily sound traveled in the house.

On the other hand, so what? She and Matt could make love quietly. Couldn't they? Even the thought caused her breath to come a little faster and desire to curl into her nether regions. She could feel her face heating and stole a glance at Matt.

What on earth would he say if he knew what she was thinking?

Matt was glad Emily had enjoyed herself tonight. He only wished he'd been able to. Unfortunately for him, the evening had been a torment.

It was a damned good thing she was due for her six-week checkup next week, because Matt knew he was almost at the end of his rope.

Finally the long-awaited and anticipated day arrived. Although originally Matt had planned to stay home and watch the baby when Emily went to the doctor, now that they knew how competent Jeff was and how well Stephanie responded to him, they decided to let Jeff do the honors.

When the time rolled around, Jeff agreed readily. "Sure. Be glad to."

So on Friday, two weeks after Jeff's arrival, Matt went off to work and left Jeff home. Emily prepared for her appointment, which was at nine o'clock. Before she left, she gave Jeff a list of instructions.

"Now don't forget to check her diaper, especially if she's fussy. She hates being wet."

"Emily, quit worrying. We'll be fine."

So Emily went off to her appointment. She had to admit it felt good to get out of the house by herself. She hadn't been alone since the baby was born, and as much as she adored little Stephanie, she missed having quiet time of her own.

Dr. Talbot pronounced her in good health. "You can now resume marital relations," he said at the end of the examination.

Ruefully, Emily wondered what he would think if he knew she and Matt had never *begun* marital relations. Nevertheless, his words excited her, even as she felt a tremor of doubt.

What if Matt no longer had any interest in making love with her? What if he was perfectly satisfied just having her as a housekeeper and companion?

That couldn't be true. Could it? Matt was a normal man, and he was only just forty-five years old— they'd celebrated his birthday in October—so surely he had a normal sex drive.

Of course, there was still the problem of Jeff, because no matter what Emily had told herself last week, upon further thought, she knew she wouldn't be comfortable making love with Matt until they once again had privacy.

But Jeff wouldn't be there forever. Even now he was looking for a place of his own. Of course, it wasn't easy finding an apartment to rent in San Pedro, but Emily had hopes it wouldn't be impossible. In fact, yesterday she had called Nell and asked her to spread the word among her patrons.

Since she was thinking of it, Emily decided to stop at Nell's salon for a minute before heading back to the house.

"Emily!" Nell said. She was cutting a woman's hair, someone Emily didn't recognize. "It's so good to see you! Where's the baby?"

"Matt's brother is baby-sitting."

Nell's face fell. "Darn."

Emily laughed. "I'm sorry. I had to go to the doctor, so I didn't want to bring her."

"So what brings you here? Do you want a haircut?

I can work you in when I'm finished with Janet. Oh, sorry. I'm forgetting my manners. Emily, this is Janet Crenshaw. She's Mrs. Braun's daughter, visiting us from Amarillo. Janet, this is Emily Thompson.''

"Hi,'' Emily said. "Nice to meet you.''

Janet Crenshaw smiled. "Nice to meet you, too.''

Emily looked at Nell again. "I know I need a haircut, but I don't have time today. No, I came in because I wondered if you'd had any luck asking about apartments.''

"No,'' Nell said. "Not so far. Rental places just don't come along very often.''

"I know,'' Emily said.

"Are you looking for someplace to rent?'' Janet Crenshaw asked.

"Not me. My brother-in-law,'' said Emily.

"Do you know of a place?'' Nell asked.

Janet nodded. "My mother's tenant is leaving the middle of the month.''

Emily's eyes widened. "Really?'' Mrs. Braun lived in one half of a duplex on Fourth Street and rented out the other half.

"Why don't you tell your brother-in-law to call her?'' Janet said.

"I will. Just as soon as I get home. Thank you!''

When Emily arrived at the house, Jeff met her at the door, putting his finger to his lips. "Stephanie just fell asleep,'' he said.

"That's good news. And now I have some good news for you.''

"Mrs. Braun?'' he said when Emily finished telling

him what Janet Crenshaw had said. "I remember her. She must be ninety by now. Lives over on Fourth Street, right?"

"That's the one," Emily said.

"Maybe I'll swing over there on my way back to the airfield."

"Good idea."

After he was gone, Emily hugged herself. Everything was working out perfectly. Cornelia was leaving them alone, the doctor had given Emily a clean bill of health and Jeff might be moving out in a week.

She couldn't wait to tell Matt.

Chapter Thirteen

"Emily, what would you say to giving Jeff your car and us buying you a new one?"

Emily and Matt had just finished dinner. The remains of the chicken, rice and broccoli casserole they'd eaten still littered the surface of the kitchen table. Stephanie, quiet and contented at the moment, was swinging in the baby swing, which Matt had brought into the kitchen.

Jeff wasn't there. Saying he'd stop and pick up a hamburger or something on his way, he'd taken the Bronco and driven into Waco to look for some inexpensive furniture to supplement the things given to him by Matt and Pam.

Emily got up and started stacking the used dishes. "I don't know. That would be all right, I guess, if you think we can afford it."

"We can afford it," Matt said. He put the top on the tub of margarine and recapped the salad dressing. "And I'd feel better if you had something sturdier and newer to drive, especially now that we've got the baby." He reached over and caressed Stephanie's cheek. He thought she was getting cuter every day.

Emily smiled and carried the dishes to the sink. "You know, Matt, it means a lot to me that you always refer to Stephanie as ours instead of just mine."

He pushed his chair back from the table and stood. "Why wouldn't I? That's how I think of her." He was telling her the truth. Although his head knew Stephen Pierce had fathered Stephanie, she had captured his heart from the first moment he held her in his arms.

"I know." Emily hesitated, then walked over to him and, standing on tiptoe, kissed his cheek. "Thanks." Before Matt could react, she turned and walked back to the sink where she began to rinse the dishes before putting them in the dishwasher.

Matt closed his eyes for a minute, because the way she looked right now in her formfitting jeans and soft sweater was doing things to him. Dangerous things. He knew he'd better be careful, otherwise he might not be able to control himself. "So what do you think about the car?" he said. His voice sounded ragged even to him.

She glanced over her shoulder. "Let's do it. Were you thinking of a brand-new car for me?"

He walked to the refrigerator and put away the margarine and salad dressing. "No, I was thinking more along the lines of a couple of years old."

"Oh."

The way she said *oh,* with that wistful sound in her voice, reminded Matt that she'd probably never had a new car. The realization made him feel bad. There were so many things Emily had never had. "On second thought," he said slowly. "It might be smarter to buy a brand-new car."

Her delighted smile was all the reward he needed.

Later, after they'd finished cleaning up the kitchen and Emily had fed Stephanie and—with crossed fingers—had put her down to sleep, Matt's thoughts once again turned to making love to Emily. He didn't want to think about it, but his mind refused to turn off. He kept imagining how it would be. How she would feel, and what it would be like to sink himself inside her warmth and make her cry out in passion.

Finally he could stand the tension pulsing through him no longer. So he told her he needed fresh air and was going out for a walk. Avoiding her curious eyes, he took his jacket out of the closet and said, "Don't wait up. I know you're tired, so you just go on to bed."

He walked several miles, and by the time he returned an hour later, Jeff was home and—Matt saw with relief—Emily had followed his suggestion. But just in case she wasn't yet asleep, he joined Jeff in the living room. Together, they watched Jay Leno on "The Tonight Show." When Matt finally went to bed, Emily was breathing evenly and deeply.

Only two more nights, Matt told himself as he gently eased himself beside her. Two more nights, then Jeff would be gone.

The following day, Matt got a call from a friend who owned a charter service in New Braunfels. "Hey, Matt," he said. "I need a favor."

Matt listened as Don explained how he had flown a charter down to Padre Island earlier in the week and how he was supposed to pick them up on Saturday to fly them back home.

"But my wife has gone into the hospital," he said, "and she's having surgery Saturday morning. Could you go down there and pick up my charter for me? I'll make it worth your while." He named a figure.

Matt thought fast. Jeff was moving on Saturday, and Matt had promised to help, but between Jeff and Ben and the boys, they ought to be able to handle it. And Matt sure could use the extra money, especially now that he wanted to get Emily a new car. "As long as I can be home Saturday night, I'll do it."

Saturday wasn't a good day for Emily. Stephanie woke up cranky, and the whole time Jeff and Ben and the boys were moving Jeff's things, the baby cried. By the time they were finished, Emily felt like crying herself.

She had so hoped to get her hair cut that afternoon. Nell said her last appointment would be gone by four o'clock and that if Emily could come in then, she'd even give her a manicure and pedicure.

"Oh, Nell," Emily had said, "I'd love to, but Matt is gone and Jeff will be moving. I won't have anyone to leave Stephanie with."

"No problem. Bring Stephanie with you."

And Emily had thought she would, but now she saw that would be impossible. She held off calling Nell, though, hoping against hope the baby would calm down. Jeff walked in just as she had given up.

"Listen, I'll watch her for you," Jeff said. "We're all done."

"Oh, Jeff, I hate to impose on you like that, especially when she's so fussy."

"C'mon, Emily, after everything you and Matt have done for me, watching Stephanie is not an imposition."

Emily wanted to. She kept thinking about Matt coming home tonight and how she'd planned to look beautiful for him. "I don't know. Maybe there's something really wrong. She hasn't cried like this for weeks."

"Gimme that kid," he said, laughing. "I'll get her settled down."

"Are you *sure?*"

"Yes, I'm sure. Now will you *go?* As long as she hears your voice, she's gonna keep crying." He reached for Stephanie.

After only a moment more of indecision, Emily gave in and handed Stephanie to him. "Now if you need me, I want you to call me. I'll write the number down by the phone, okay?"

"I'm not going to need you." He held Stephanie

upright, against his left shoulder, and patted her back, making soothing noises as he did.

"Well, if you do..."

Jeff rolled his eyes. "Emily, will you get *out* of here? I'm not going to get her quieted down until you're gone."

Cornelia was riding off some of her frustration over O'Malley's silence on the back of a new dapple gray she'd purchased the week before. She and the horse had both worked up a good sweat, and Cornelia felt better, so she turned the horse toward home.

O'Malley had been gone more than a week now, and she hadn't heard from him since the night he arrived in L.A. What was the man doing? She had half a notion to call him up and fire him. She was beginning to think he was stringing this investigation out just so he could take more of her money.

Her thoughts continued along in this vein until she cantered over the north ridge, then they abruptly stopped as she spied Rosella standing by the entrance to the stables.

"That Mr. O'Malley called," Rosella said as Cornelia dismounted. "He wants you to call him back. Says it's important."

Cornelia's pulse rate accelerated as excitement raced through her. He must have good news, otherwise he would not have said it was important. After turning the horse over to one of the hands, she stalked off toward the house. Her hands were shaking as she dialed the California number.

The phone only rang twice before he answered, saying, "O'Malley."

"This is Cornelia Pierce. What have you got for me?"

"Pay dirt. The trouble Jeff Thompson was in out here was prison."

Her heart jumped. "Prison!"

"Uh-huh."

Cornelia listened as he explained. When they hung up ten minutes later, she smiled triumphantly. Now she had exactly what she needed. Her granddaughter was living in the same house as an ex-convict!

Hurriedly she cleaned up and changed into fresh clothes. Then, telling Rosella she'd be gone for a while, she walked out to the garage, started the Buick and headed toward town.

Matt was pleased with himself. The charter had gone well, he'd gotten his money from Don and now he was on his way home. He'd easily make it to the house by five.

Tonight, he kept thinking. *Tonight.*

He couldn't wait.

"Oh, I love it!" Emily said in delight. Nell had talked her into cutting her hair a little shorter than she normally wore it, and now it just skimmed the bottom of her chin. "I wish I knew how to style it like you do." She turned to look at the back.

"It's all in the way you dry it. Well, and plus you've got to have the right styling brush," Nell said.

"Tell you what. You buy one of these brushes, and I'll show you how to use it. But let's do your nails first."

"No, first I think I should call home and see if everything's all right."

"Emily, for heaven's sake. Jeff's a smart guy. He knows enough to call you if he needs you. Now will you please just *relax?*"

Feeling sheepish, Emily walked to the manicure table and sat across from Nell.

"What you need," Nell said, laughing, "is a few more kids. Believe me, once you have two or three, you quit worrying about every little squeak they make."

"This is more than squeaking, Nell. She cried all day long."

"Well, forget about it for now. Let's make you beautiful for that husband of yours."

Emily couldn't help smiling.

Tonight was the night.

Oh, she so wanted it to be perfect. She had it all planned. She'd gotten filet mignon at the butcher shop and had splurged on fresh asparagus and tiny new potatoes at the Piggly Wiggly. She also had some scented candles she'd been saving for a special occasion, and if this wasn't special, she didn't know what was.

Please God, she prayed, *please let Stephanie go to sleep early and let her sleep for at least a couple of hours. And most of all, please help me not to disappoint Matt.*

* * *

It took Jeff forty minutes to get Stephanie to stop crying. And then, just as he was about to lay her down in her crib, her eyes popped open, and she let out an earsplitting shriek.

He tried everything. Changing her diaper. Giving her the pacifier. Bouncing her up and down. Singing to her. Rocking her.

Nothing worked.

She cried so hard she became hoarse, and still she cried.

Reluctantly he headed for the phone. Maybe he'd better call Emily.

Cornelia heard the baby crying the minute she stepped out of her truck. She hurried to the front door and rang the bell. Waited. Rang it again. The baby kept crying. What were they *doing* to her grandchild?

Finally the front door opened.

A younger version of Matt, a harried look in his eyes, held the screaming baby in his arms. He was patting her and bouncing her, but she continued to wail at the top of her lungs. This was Matt's brother Jeff—no doubt about it.

He frowned at Cornelia. "Can I help you?" He had to raise his voice to be heard over Stephanie's cries.

"I am Cornelia Pierce, Stephanie's grandmother," Cornelia announced haughtily. "I wish to speak with Emily."

"I'm sorry, Mrs. Pierce. I didn't recognize you. Emily's not here." He continued to bounce Stephanie, to no avail. "Shhh, shhh." He stood back politely. "Would you like to come in? Emily will back soon."

Cornelia brushed past him. "What do you mean, she's not here? Where is she?"

"She's getting her hair cut."

"Getting her hair cut! You mean she left the baby with *you?*"

He stiffened. "Look, I'm doing my best. I don't know why Stephanie won't stop crying. The other times I've watched her, she's been fine."

Why, it was worse than Cornelia had imagined. Not only was her granddaughter living in the same house with an ex-convict, her mother had entrusted her care to him. And more than once! Cornelia couldn't believe it. Stephanie was only six weeks old. Much too young to be left in the care of someone else, unless that someone else was a trained nurse!

Cornelia felt like grabbing the baby and leaving. Getting Stephanie away from this totally unsuitable, even possibly *dangerous* environment. Yes, that's exactly what she should do, she thought in mounting excitement. That's what Stephen would have wanted, she just knew it. Yet Cornelia was shrewd enough to know she couldn't let her outrage or her intentions show. Using her considerable strength of will, she eliminated all traces of disapproval from her voice. "Let me have her. I can calm her down." She reached for Stephanie.

After a moment of hesitation, he relinquished his hold on the baby. In surprise—or maybe because she was finally exhausted—Stephanie stopped crying and stared up at Cornelia. Cornelia cradled her close, drinking in every feature on her tiny face. And as she studied her granddaughter, something happened to her. The pain and emptiness that had frozen her heart the day Stephen died melted away as if it had never existed.

Her decision made, Cornelia tightened her arms around Stephanie and walked out the front door.

"Wait a minute!" Jeff said, running after Cornelia. He grabbed her arm. "Where are you going?"

Cornelia turned and gave him her coldest look. "Take your hand off me."

Jeff started to say something, obviously thought better of it and removed his hand.

Cornelia opened the back door of her car. She congratulated herself on her foresight, for a week ago she'd purchased a car seat and had installed it. She placed Stephanie in the seat and buckled her in.

"Where are you taking her?" Jeff said.

Without looking at him, she said, "You may inform your brother and his wife that I have taken my granddaughter home—where she belongs. She certainly does *not* belong in the care of an ex-convict, and if they had the sense they were born with, they'd know that." And then she climbed into the driver's seat, shut the door, started the car and backed out of the driveway.

Seconds later, she was gone.

Nell finished Emily's right hand and was just starting on her left when the phone rang.

"Aren't you going to answer that?" Emily said when it had rung several times.

"It's after-hours. I think I'll just let the answering machine pick up."

"But it might be Jeff."

Nell sighed and shook her head. "Okay, okay." She put down the nail polish and walked over to the phone. She picked it up and listened a moment. Then she held out the receiver. "It *is* Jeff."

Emily jumped up, nearly upsetting the manicure table in her haste. She grabbed the phone. "Jeff? What's wrong?"

"Emily, you've got to come home right now. Cornelia Pierce was just here. And she took Stephanie. I couldn't stop her." There was an undercurrent of panic in his voice.

Emily's heart shot into her throat. "Ohmigod! I'll be right there!" She dropped the phone and looked around frantically for her purse.

"What happened?" Nell said.

"Oh, Nell." Fear caused her voice to shake. "Where's my purse? I've got to go. Cornelia Pierce has taken Stephanie!"

Nell dashed over to her hair station and took Emily's purse from the shelf where she'd put it earlier. Emily grabbed it and raced out the door.

She drove home blindly and much too fast, but she got there without having an accident. When she pulled in the drive, Jeff was standing outside, waiting for her.

"Emily, I'm sorry," he said.

By now Emily had calmed down a little bit. Cornelia wasn't going to hurt Stephanie, she knew that. And she wasn't going to spirit the baby away somewhere. At least, Emily didn't think she would. No, surely Cornelia would take the baby out to the ranch. So all Emily had to do was go out there and get Stephanie. But, oh God, she wished Matt were here. She knew she was no match for Cornelia by herself, and she had a feeling Jeff wasn't, either. Otherwise he never would have let Cornelia take Stephanie in the first place. Yet how could she blame him? He knew nothing of the situation. Belatedly she realized they should have told him all about Cornelia so he would have been prepared. Instead, they'd been lulled into thinking their problems with her were over.

"Short of attacking her, I couldn't stop her," he said, just as if he knew what Emily was thinking.

Emily took a deep breath. She had to remain calm. "I know that, Jeff. I'm not blaming you. Now tell me exactly what happened."

He was in the middle of his explanation when Matt's Bronco turned the corner. Relief caused Emily's knees to feel weak, and she leaned against the car.

Matt parked the Bronco behind her car and got out. "What's wrong?" he said, walking rapidly toward them.

So Jeff started from the beginning. By the time he got to the part about Cornelia taking Stephanie, Matt's face had turned to stone. Emily realized he was furious, and knowing this, she suddenly felt calmer.

With Matt at her side, nothing bad would happen, because he wouldn't let it.

"C'mon," Matt said, taking Emily's arm. "Let's go." When Jeff started toward the truck, too, Matt said, "I don't think you should come with us, seeing how she feels about you, Jeff."

Jeff visibly flinched.

Emily felt bad for Jeff, because she could see he was hurt, but right now she couldn't worry about Jeff's feelings. Stephanie was what was important, and if Matt felt having Jeff with them would make dealing with Cornelia more difficult, then she didn't want him there.

They didn't talk as they drove to the ranch. Each was lost in their own thoughts. Each was berating themselves for things done and not done. Each was praying there would be no trouble when they got there.

"You *what?*" Walker Nesbitt shouted.

"I said, I took the baby. She's here with me now," Cornelia said calmly.

After a few seconds of pregnant silence, Walker said in a quieter voice, "Cornelia, you can't keep her. You do realize that, don't you?"

"I realize nothing of the sort." Cornelia hated that her voice trembled. She hated that she hadn't gone more than a mile after leaving Emily and Matt's house before the doubts had set in. She hated that Walker was probably right. She glanced down at Stephanie, who was lying quietly in the middle of

Cornelia's bed. Her green eyes—exactly like Stephen's—studied Cornelia gravely. Cornelia swallowed against the lump in her throat. Tears blurred her eyes. *Stephen...oh, Stephen....*

"Cornelia..." he said softly.

Hot tears coursed down her cheeks. Without answering, she hung up the phone.

The drive seemed to take hours, even though they pulled through the entrance archway leading to the main house less than fifteen minutes from the time they left their house.

"Matt," Emily said, "what if she won't let us have Stephanie? Maybe we should have called Sheriff Krell."

"We don't need Sheriff Krell," Matt said tightly. "I'll take care of this."

A few minutes later, the ranch house and surrounding outbuildings came into view. As they drove closer, Emily could see a tall figure standing in the yard.

Cornelia.

Myriad emotions passed through Emily. She was no longer afraid. They would get Stephanie, if not this minute, then very soon, because the law was on their side. But she was filled with an aching sadness. How had things progressed to this point? She and Cornelia were Stephanie's only two blood relatives. They should be able to love her and share her, not fight over her.

Matt parked the Bronco alongside several trucks.

By the time he'd gotten out and walked around to Emily's side, she was already climbing down. Together, they walked toward Cornelia, who held Stephanie in her arms.

Cornelia stepped forward, and for one long moment her glittering green eyes locked with Emily's. And then, wordlessly, she handed Stephanie into Emily's arms.

Chapter Fourteen

Emily didn't fall apart until they were once again in the safety of their own home. Jeff—still apologizing—had left to go to his apartment and a sleeping Stephanie was safely tucked away in her crib.

Then, and only then, did she break down in a delayed reaction.

"Ah, sweetheart," Matt said, enfolding her into his arms. "Don't." He held her close, caressing her hair and cheeks. He kissed the top of her head. Her entire body was trembling, making him feel helpless. "Everything's okay now. Everything's fine."

God, he loved her so much. He couldn't stand it when she cried. He wanted to keep everything bad away from her. He wanted to see only smiles on her face and happiness in her eyes.

She clung to him, crying her heart out. Finally, after a long time, her tears slowed, then stopped altogether. She took a long, shaky breath and raised her face. "I'm sorry. I don't know what's the matter with me. I—I don't know why I'm crying."

Tenderness filled him. Her eyes were all puffy and her nose was red, but she was still the most beautiful sight in all the world. "There's nothing to be sorry about. You're crying because it's a natural release of tension. Hell..." He made a self-mocking grimace. "If I wasn't a big, strong man, I'd probably be crying myself."

His words had the desired effect, because she laughed sheepishly. Then the smile disappeared and, in a steadier voice, she said, "It's just that I was so frightened."

"I know. So was I."

"Were you? You didn't act as if you were."

"That was just a front so *you* wouldn't be worried." He grinned. "You know, *big, strong man...*"

This time she didn't smile. "Oh, Matt, what if..."

"Shhh. No what-ifs. Nothing happened. You're fine, I'm fine, Stephanie's fine. And we're all home again. Together."

"Together," she whispered.

Their eyes met, held. A man could happily drown in those eyes, he thought. There was something...some emotion in her eyes he'd never seen there before. For a long moment, it immobilized him. And then, her gaze still locked to his, she whispered his name. The sound galvanized him, and no longer able to deny the love so long suppressed, he lowered his mouth to hers.

At first it was a gentle kiss, just a grazing of his lips against hers. But then she sighed and moved in closer, wrapping her arms around his waist. Her mouth opened under his, and from that moment on Matt was lost.

"Emily," he said raggedly, kissing her again and again. She was so sweet. So sweet. His mouth plundered hers until the passion raging through him had ignited into an inferno of need. He wanted her so much. Yet still he hesitated. He had to be sure. Dragging his mouth from hers, he searched her eyes. "You know what I want?"

She nodded slowly.

"I want to make love to you." He had to spell it out, because there could not be any misunderstandings. He wanted her, yes, but he wanted her with her full knowledge and consensus.

"Yes," she said. "I know."

The next few seconds stretched into infinity.

And then she smiled. "That's what I want, too."

Matt's heart soared. As if she weighed nothing, he swooped her up and carried her into their bedroom.

He could hardly believe his long wait was almost over.

At the first touch of Matt's lips, happiness flooded Emily. Yes. Yes. This was what she'd been waiting for and longing for. This was what she needed so desperately. She closed her eyes, put her arms around him and returned his kisses with eagerness and abandon.

With each kiss, her blood ran faster, her heart pumped harder and her need for him grew stronger. She melted against him, all liquid heat and desire, her body pliant and ready for him to claim.

And now, at long last, it was going to happen. They were going to seal their union. They were going to become husband and wife in every way that mattered.

When he picked her up, Emily laid her head against his chest and closed her eyes. She loved his strength and the way he had taken charge, both earlier today with Cornelia and now...with her.

Once inside the bedroom, he gently set her down, but continued to hold her close. He kissed her again, feathering her face and then her neck, finally dropping his warm, moist lips into the crevice between her breasts.

She swallowed, closing her eyes and absorbing the lovely sensations as his hands explored, stroking her bottom and holding it close so that she could feel his arousal against her, then moving up and around to cup her breasts. When, with his thumbs, he gently skimmed over her nipples, desire arrowed through her. She moaned. It felt so good to have him touch her. So good.

With unsteady hands, he began to unbutton her blouse. After a second or two, Emily helped him. It took them a few fumbling tries, but they eventually managed to get rid of their clothes.

Abruptly, shyness attacked Emily, and doubts assailed her. Matt hadn't ever seen her completely naked before. What if she disappointed him? She wished it was dark. She wished he couldn't see her body. She wished she'd had a chance to put on cologne and her pretty blue nightgown. She was a mess, she was sure of it. Her hair was probably wild by now, and after that crying jag she could just imagine how awful her face looked.

As if he knew every one of her negative thoughts, he put his hand under her chin and raised her face. "You're so beautiful, Emily. So very beautiful."

"I—I'm not."

"I think you're beautiful."

Oh, Matt...

"Stand back," he whispered. "Let me really look at you."

His eyes swept her slowly.

Emily didn't want to, but she couldn't help wondering how she measured up against his first wife. *What if he thinks he's made a bad bargain?*

Because she knew thoughts like this were only going to make her more nervous, she tried to distract herself by looking at Matt. She had to admit, she was curious about his body, too, because she'd never seen him completely naked, either.

He had a wonderful body, she decided. Broad through the shoulders, narrow through the hips, with just enough muscle definition in his chest, but not too much. With relief, she realized Matt's body was very different from Stephen's, but just as sexy. Maybe even more so, with its line of golden chest hair that arrowed down to...Emily swallowed as her eyes were irresistibly drawn downward. Her heart thudded as she saw just how much he wanted her, and she quickly looked away. What if she couldn't satisfy him? What if, after they made love, he was sorry he'd married her? Confused by her conflicting emotions and the doubts assailing her, she avoided his eyes.

He put his arms around her again. Feeling her stiffness, he said, "You're not afraid, are you?"

"No." She licked her lips. "Not really."

"Not really? What does that mean?"

She wanted to tell him, yet she didn't want him to know.

"I won't hurt you," he said, misunderstanding her silence.

"It's not that," she blurted out. "I—I'm just afraid I'll disappoint you."

He stared at her. He seemed to be struggling with something. Finally he said, "Emily, I love you. Don't you know that? You could never disappoint me."

The words shimmered in the air between them, stunning her. "You...you love me?"

He closed his eyes, leaning his forehead against hers. "I'm sorry. I never meant to say that. I vowed I'd never put this kind of pressure on you. Look, I know you don't love me, and that's okay."

"Oh, Matt."

He looked at her again. "And I don't want you feeling sorry for me, either. I told you. It's okay. I can live without you loving me."

But she *did* love Matt! She did! She guessed she'd

loved him for a long time now, but, until this moment, she hadn't realized it. "Oh, Matt. My darling Matt. I *do* love you. I love you so much."

Emily knew she would never forget the joy that lit Matt's face as the import of her words really sank in.

He kissed her then, holding her face between his hands. The kiss was soft, almost reverent, as if she were a fragile piece of crystal.

When it ended, he lifted her to the bed, laying her down tenderly, then he lay beside her. Propping himself on one elbow, he began to stroke her and kiss her until her fears vanished and her body was once more languid and floating with sensation.

At first, she tried to touch him, too. "Not yet," he murmured. "Not yet."

Finally he reached for her hand and guided it to him. She closed her palm around him, reveling in the groan he made no attempt to suppress. She loved touching him, she discovered, but when she would have explored his body further, he abruptly pushed her hand away.

Afraid she'd done something wrong, she said, "What's the matter?"

"Oh, Emily," he said with a groan. "Nothing's the matter. But if you keep touching me like that, I won't be able to wait." He leaned over her. "I want this to be good for you." He cupped one of her breasts, then lowered his mouth to the hard little peak. "Very good."

When his mouth closed over her nipple, Emily cried out.

"Shh," he said, moving to the other breast. "Shh."

"I need...I want..." She gasped as his teeth gently nipped while his fingers searched, then delved into the place where all the needing and wanting was centered.

"Easy," he murmured, his mouth moving lower. "Easy." His fingers circled, then applied more pressure.

"Matt..." Emily's body bowed. She was too close. Too close. Soon she would have no control left.

"Let yourself go," he whispered.

Emily was lost. She couldn't have stopped him if she'd wanted to, even though in some part of her mind she felt this glorious abandonment to her own pleasure had to be selfish. That was her last coherent thought, for within minutes he brought her to the brink, and seconds later she plunged over in an explosion of pleasure so intense she was sure she would die of it.

It was only then, when her shuddering began to subside, that he lifted himself over her and, smiling down into her eyes, he parted her thighs and entered her, pushing deep.

She cried out, not because he was hurting her, but because it felt so good and so right to have him there, sunk deep inside, filling her in every way that mattered.

My love, she thought as he pushed even deeper. She lifted to meet him, matching her movements to his.

Unbelievably her body responded, and that exquisite tension that was half agony, half ecstasy, began to build again. She clutched his back, feeling his muscles ripple under her palms as they moved faster and faster.

And then he gave a great shudder, and his body erupted into hers. Emily held on tight as another shattering climax left her breathless.

Afterward, lying quietly in his arms, his lips pressed against her forehead, she was filled with such happiness, it scared her. She had thought Stephen was the great love of her life, but she'd been wrong. She'd loved Stephen, yes, and she would always love him, because he'd been her first love.

But Matt...Matt was her destiny.

And today was just the beginning.

She and Matt would build a wonderful life together, a splendid life filled with more children and work they enjoyed and friends and family and hundreds of memories.

Their love would withstand any obstacles or adversity placed in its path.

They would grow old together, and their love would endure, growing stronger with each passing year.

And it was with this quiet conviction filling her heart that she finally drifted off into sleep.

Matt watched Emily sleep. He was certain he would never tire of looking at her. He knew he certainly would never tire of making love to her. Just thinking about how good it had been made him want to make love to her again. But she needed her sleep. Stephanie could wake at any moment.

But even as he thought so, Emily stirred and snuggled deeper into his arms. "Matt," she murmured sleepily.

"What, my darling?"

"I'm so happy."

He smiled, kissing the tip of her nose. "I'm glad."

"Are you happy?"

He chuckled. "If I were any happier, they'd probably have to put me in a straitjacket, because I'd be dancing in the streets and acting like a world-class idiot."

She sighed. A few minutes later, she said, "When did you first know you loved me?"

"The very first time I set eyes on you."

"Really?" Now her eyes opened fully and she drew back a little to look at him.

"Really."

She thought about that for a while, then said thoughtfully, "But if you loved me then...how did you feel when I...when I met Stephen?"

He traced the curve of her cheek, tucking a strand of hair behind her ears. "At first? Complete and utter despair." He sighed, remembering. "But later on? Resignation. And, to be completely honest, I was angry, too. At myself, mostly." He grimaced. "At the fates."

"Oh, Matt...I had no idea."

"If you had, would it have made any difference?"

She was quiet for a long moment. "I have to be

honest, too. No, it probably wouldn't have made any difference, then. But that was because I didn't know what I know now.''

''Which is?''

She caressed his cheek. ''That we were meant for each other.''

He covered her hand with his.

''Stephen will always occupy a special place in my heart,'' she continued softly. ''He was my first love and he's the father of my child. But this love...*our* love, oh, Matt, I really feel it's a gift from God. That *you're* a gift from God. You've made me happier than I ever thought I could be.''

Her words touched something deep inside Matt. They made him feel humble, yet proud. And they filled him with thankfulness, because no matter what Emily said, she and Stephanie were the true gifts.

And he was the luckiest man on earth.

Epilogue

The following October

Emily finished fluting the birthday cake, and put down the paper cone of pink frosting. She looked at Matt who was standing on a ladder stringing balloons across the ceiling. They were getting ready for Stephanie's first birthday party.

"Do you think she'll come?"

He stopped and looked down at her. "Probably not."

Emily nodded. Matt hadn't wanted her to invite Cornelia to Stephanie's birthday party. After all, he'd said—several times—Cornelia had never apologized for the things she'd said and done, not even for taking

Stephanie on that fateful day last November. It was the first time since Emily and Matt were married that they'd had any kind of disagreement.

"Emily," he'd said. "She wouldn't even talk to you when you called her. Why would you want to invite her to Stephanie's party?"

True enough, Emily thought, remembering how, a few days after Cornelia's attempted abduction of Stephanie, Emily had called the ranch in an effort to bury the hatchet.

"I'm really sorry, Mrs. Thompson," the housekeeper had said. "But Miz Pierce..." She lowered her voice. "She's a stubborn old lady, and she says she doesn't want to talk to you. I think she's too embarrassed by what she did."

Emily hid her astonishment at the housekeeper's unprecedented willingness to talk about Cornelia. She thanked Rosella and hung up.

A few months later, she'd tried again. Her thinking then was that maybe now that there was some distance between the episode and her attempt at conciliation, Cornelia might respond more positively.

The older woman refused to come to the phone.

In the spring, Emily sent Cornelia a birthday card from Stephanie, with a picture enclosed.

There was no response.

And now she'd sent her an invitation to Stephanie's birthday party.

"I guess I don't understand why you keep trying," Matt said, climbing down from the ladder. "She's made it clear how she feels."

"I know, but I'm so happy, Matt, that I hate to see her so unhappy. And she *is* Stephanie's grandmother. The only grandparent she's got that's still living. Don't you think we owe it to Stephanie to do everything we can to see that she has the opportunity to get to know her grandmother?"

"Ah, Emily, you're such a softie." He walked over to her and put his arms around her. It was a bit difficult to hug him back since her stomach protruded quite a bit now that she was almost seven months pregnant.

"How's our son doing today?" Matt said after he kissed her. He touched the top of her stomach.

Emily smiled. "He's been moving around quite a bit. I think he's getting impatient."

Just then, Stephanie, who was sitting in her high chair, banged her spoon against her tray. "Ma Ma Ma Ma," she said in her sweet baby voice.

"Speaking of impatient," Emily said, laughing, "the birthday girl calls."

"You go take care of her, and I'll finish up the party preparations," Matt said.

An hour later, everything was ready and the first guests arrived—Pam, Ben and their boys, laden down with presents. Ben, Jr., headed straight for Stephanie, picking her up out of her walker and giving her a hug. She laughed delightedly. She adored Ben, Jr.

Soon after, Jeff and his "main squeeze"—as he teasingly put it—showed up. Ironically he had met and begun to date Brenda Colby six months earlier, and now it looked as if they were really serious about each other. Emily couldn't help wondering how Cornelia felt about that, because she knew Cornelia had harbored hopes Brenda would be her own daughter-in-law. At first, Emily worried about Jeff, afraid he'd be hurt, afraid Brenda might be toying with him. But after meeting Brenda and seeing her with Jeff, Emily had relaxed. Brenda was a nice woman, and it was obvious to anyone with half an eye that she was crazy about Jeff.

In short order, the rest of the guests came: Nell and her husband and several of their younger children, a couple of the guys who worked for Matt and their wives, and a few of Emily's and Matt's other friends and their children.

Every time the doorbell rang, Emily held her breath. But it was never Cornelia. And when the birthday party had been in full swing for about an hour, she knew Cornelia wasn't going to come.

Swallowing her disappointment, she decided she had done all she could. If Cornelia wanted nothing to do with them, nothing to do with *Stephanie,* it was her loss.

And then, just when she had finally put Cornelia out of her mind, the doorbell pealed again.

Matt had just lighted the candle on Stephanie's cake. He looked at Emily. Emily, pulse picking up speed, walked to the door. She opened it, and her eyes met a familiar gleam of green.

After her shock subsided, Emily smiled. "Hello, Mrs. Pierce."

Cornelia, with a touch of defiance—because, after

all, a leopard doesn't change its spots overnight—said, "Hello, Emily. Am I still welcome here?"

"Of course you are. Please. Come in."

Head held high, Cornelia entered.

All activity in the room ceased. Mouths agape, everyone fell silent, even Stephanie, who stopped in mid-giggle and stared at the newcomer.

Cornelia's gaze moved to her granddaughter and, before Emily's eyes, her defiant stance crumpled. There was an expression of such poignancy and sadness on her face that Emily's tender heart constricted. Impulsively, not even thinking that she might be rebuffed, she put her arm around Cornelia's shoulders.

"Come," she said softly, "I think your granddaughter wants to see you."

Later, Emily would realize how Matt, at that moment, began to shepherd the other guests out of the living room so that Emily, Cornelia and Stephanie could have some privacy. But right then, Emily was too concentrated on helping her former mother-in-law through this emotional moment and on trying to keep her own emotions from skittering out of control.

Picking Stephanie up, Emily placed her in Cornelia's arms. Closing her eyes, Cornelia held the baby close.

Emily swallowed, her own eyes filling with tears.

A moment later, Cornelia opened her eyes. They were suspiciously bright. "Emily." Her voice sounded strained. "What I did. It was wrong. But I thought I was doing the right thing. I only wanted the best for Stephen's daughter."

"I know."

"I'm sorry."

A lesser woman might have extracted her pound of flesh, but Emily was too kind and too generous. So she walked forward and put her arms around Cornelia and said, "I'm glad you're here."

Later, after the other guests returned, and the cake was relighted, and they'd sung "Happy Birthday," her eyes met Matt's. In them, she saw love, but she also saw something else: admiration, respect and pride.

Her heart swelled. Her life was so wonderful that it sometimes scared her. A silent prayer ran through her mind.

Dearest Lord, thank You for all my blessings. I will be eternally grateful, and I will never take them for granted.

And then, with a happy smile, she joined her husband across the room.

* * * * *

MARIE FERRARELLA's

miniseries continues with her brand-new Silhouette single title

In The Family Way

Dr. Rafe Saldana was Bedford's most popular pediatrician. And though the handsome doctor had a whole lot of love for his tiny patients, his heart wasn't open for business with women. At least, not until single mother Dana Morrow walked into his life. But Dana was about to become the newest member of the Baby of the Month Club. Was the dashing doctor ready to play daddy to her baby-to-be?

Available June 1998.

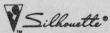

Find this new title by Marie Ferrarella
at your favorite retail outlet.

Look us up on-line at: http://www.romance.net   PSMFIFWAY

MEN at WORK
All work and no play? Not these men!

April 1998
KNIGHT SPARKS by Mary Lynn Baxter
Sexy lawman Rance Knight made a career of arresting the bad guys. Somehow, though, he thought policewoman Carly Mitchum was framed. Once they'd uncovered the truth, could Rance let Carly go...or would he make a citizen's arrest?

May 1998
HOODWINKED by Diana Palmer
CEO Jake Edwards donned coveralls and went undercover as a mechanic to find the saboteur in his company. Nothing— or no one—would distract him, not even beautiful secretary Maureen Harris. Jake had to catch the thief—*and* the woman who'd stolen his heart!

June 1998
DEFYING GRAVITY by Rachel Lee
Tim O'Shaughnessy and his business partner, Liz Pennington, had always been close—but never *this* close. As the danger of their assignment escalated, so did their passion. When the job was over, could they ever go back to business as usual?

MEN AT WORK™

Available at your favorite retail outlet!

 HARLEQUIN®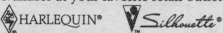

Look us up on-line at: http://www.romance.net   PMAW1

BEVERLY BARTON

Continues the twelve-book series— 36 Hours—in April 1998 with Book Ten

NINE MONTHS

Paige Summers couldn't have been more shocked when she learned that the man with whom she had spent one passionate, stormy night was none other than her arrogant new boss! And just because he was the father of her unborn baby didn't give him the right to claim her as his wife. Especially when he wasn't offering the one thing she wanted: his heart.

For Jared and Paige and *all* the residents of Grand Springs, Colorado, the storm-induced blackout was just the beginning of 36 Hours that changed *everything!* You won't want to miss a single book.

Available at your favorite retail outlet.

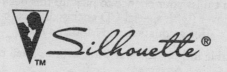

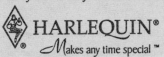

COMING NEXT MONTH

#1171 UNEXPECTED MOMMY—Sherryl Woods
That Special Woman!
And Baby Makes Three: The Next Generation
Single father Chance Adams was hell-bent on claiming his share of
the family ranch. Even if it meant trying to seduce his uncle's lovely
stepdaughter. But when Chance fell in love with the spirited beauty for real,
could he convince Jenny to be his wife—and his son's new mommy?

#1172 A FATHER'S VOW—Myrna Temte
Montana Mavericks: Return to Whitehorn
Traditional Native American Sam Brightwater was perfectly content
with his life. Until vivacious schoolteacher Julia Stedman stormed into
Whitehorn and wrapped herself around his hardened heart. With fatherhood
beckoning, Sam vowed to swallow his pride and fight for his woman and
child....

#1173 STALLION TAMER—Lindsay McKenna
Cowboys of the Southwest
Vulnerable Jessica Donovan sought solace on the home front, but what she
found was a soul mate in lone horse wrangler Dan Black. She identified
with the war veteran's pain, as well as with the secret yearning in his eyes.
Would the healing force of their love grant them a beautiful life together?

#1174 PRACTICALLY MARRIED—Christine Rimmer
Conveniently Yours
Rancher Zach Bravo vowed to never get burned by a woman again. But he
knew that soft-spoken single mom Tess DeMarley would be the perfect
wife. And he was positively *livid* at the notion that Tess's heart belonged to
someone else. Could he turn this practical union into a true love match?

#1175 THE PATERNITY QUESTION—Andrea Edwards
Double Wedding
Sophisticated city-dweller Neal Sheridan was elated when he secretly
swapped places with his country-based twin. Until he accidentally agreed to
father gorgeous Lisa Hughes's child! He had no intention of fulfilling that
promise, but could he really resist Lisa's baby-making seduction?

#1176 BABY IN HIS CRADLE—Diana Whitney
Stork Express
On the run from her manipulative ex, very pregnant Ellie Malone wound up
on the doorstep of Samuel Evans's mountain retreat. When the brooding
recluse delivered her baby and tenderly nursed her back to health, her heart
filled with hope. Would love bring joy and laughter back into their lives?